"I'm aware of my strengths as well as my faults."

"Name one. A fault, I mean," Maeve challenged.

Victor stepped close and placed his mouth to her ear. "I can't seem to get you off my mind."

"That's a fault?"

"Right now, to be honest, it's one hell of a problem. I very much want to get to know you better, but there's a lawsuit in the way."

"Which is why, as much as I have enjoyed the evening, I think we should limit all future interactions to the courtroom."

"Are you sure about that?"

"Positive."

"For now, I'll abide by your wishes, Maeve Eddington. But after winning this case, I'm taking you out, a proper date."

"After losing this case, you might change your mind."

"I won't."

"Lose, or change your mind?"

"Neither."

"We'll see."

* * *

Two Rivals, One Bed by Zuri Day is part of The Eddington Heirs series.

Dear Reader,

One Love, beautiful reader! I trust this letter finds you well and thriving as collectively we navigate a postpandemic world. There's nothing like a good ole rivalry between mutually attracted souls to set up a temporary page-turning escape from the absurdity, a chance to remember that love conquers all. That's what happens when attorney Maeve Eddington finds herself across the courtroom aisle from a college acquaintance, Victor Cortez. Outwardly, there is a continual verbal battle as both work to win the case, but just beneath the surface, and not too far down, simmers a fire of desire that eventually must be quenched.

Developing Victor's backstory allowed me the chance to luxuriate in one of my fondest travel memories—two glorious weeks spent in Costa Rica as part of an eight-day Indian wedding celebration. That paradise, specifically Uvita, immediately became one of my favorite places on earth. The incredible beauty. The culture. The nature. The peace. If you've never visited CR, I highly recommend it. While there, be sure to also visit Puerto Limón, a township filled with a colorful history and part of Victor's roots. Until next time, dear DayDreamers, enjoy their story and remember to have a zuri day!

Zuri

ZURI DAY

TWO RIVALS, ONE BED

HARLEQUIN®
DESIRE™

Recycling programs
for this product may
not exist in your area.

ISBN-13: 978-1-335-58154-9

Two Rivals, One Bed

Copyright © 2022 by Zuri Day

For questions and comments about the quality of this book, please contact us at CustomerService@Harlequin.com.

Harlequin Enterprises ULC
22 Adelaide St. West, 41st Floor
Toronto, Ontario M5H 4E3, Canada
www.Harlequin.com

Printed in U.S.A.

Zuri Day is the award-winning, nationally bestselling author of a slew of novels translated into almost a dozen languages. When not writing, which is almost never, or traveling internationally, these days not so much, she can be found in the weeds, literally, engaged in her latest passion—gardening. Living in Southern California, this happens year-round. From there it's farm to table (okay, patio to table—it's an urban garden) via her creative culinary take on a variety of vegan dishes. She loves live performances (including her own), binges on popular YouTube shows and is diligently at work to make her Ragdoll cat, Namaste, the IG star he deserves to be. Say meow to him, stay in touch with her and check out her exhaustive stash of OMG reads at zuriday.com.

Books by Zuri Day

Harlequin Desire

The Eddington Heirs

Inconvenient Attraction
The Nanny Game
Two Rivals, One Bed

Sin City Secrets

Sin City Vows
Ready for the Rancher
Sin City Seduction
The Last Little Secret

Visit her Author Profile page at Harlequin.com, or zuriday.com, for more titles.

You can also find Zuri Day on Facebook, along with other Harlequin Desire authors, at Facebook.com/harlequindesireauthors!

An attraction between rivals
causes infinite drama

Especially when stoked by emotional trauma

But progress is made
when animosities fade, so that

They can sleep together in
the bed that life made.

One

When Maeve Eddington graduated Harvard Law School, she returned to Chicago to work for and be mentored by Eleanor Buchanan, a legend in corporate law. Buchanan's motto: Be Tough Enough That Men Forget You're a Woman. She fashioned herself as "one of the boys," her closet filled with plain, shapeless suits in navy, gray, brown and black. No other colors. No exceptions. During her first two years at Buchanan and Bausch, Maeve followed that lead of conservative dress. One morning, as she joined her mother for tea before heading into the office, Mona asked a question. "When did you change professions?"

Maeve was confused. "What do you mean?"

Mona's eyes traveled the length of her and back, taking in the black pantsuit paired with a black turtleneck and pearls, low-heeled black pumps and hair pulled tight at the nape of her neck.

"You're an attorney, but you're dressed like a funeral director."

"It's called fitting in," Maeve said amid relieved laughter. "Eleanor says it's important to blend in as one of the boys."

Mona nodded slowly, thoughtfully sipping her tea. "I'm no law expert, but I know a thing or two about men, and being a woman among them."

She placed her hand over her daughter's and looked her straight in the eye. "Your name isn't Eleanor. It's Maeve. You're a beautiful woman whose femininity should be embraced, not obscured. It is a powerful weapon, not a weakness but a strength. It is the woman's hand that rocks cradles and rules nations. Wielded skillfully, thoughtfully, it can dominate in boardrooms and courtrooms, too."

Mona never again brought up the subject. The following week, however, Maeve returned home to find a garment bag hanging at the front of her walk-in closet. Inside was a suit, powder blue, with a respectful yet sexy peekaboo split that stopped just below the thigh. Below the bag was a pair of her favorite red-bottomed shoes, navy, with bows covered in crystals and five-inch heels. Her mother knew her daughter's taste. Maeve loved the outfit. The next day, she wore it. When she entered the boardroom for the firm's morning meeting, the women sputtered. The men all paused. Maeve commanded attention without saying a word. Her peers were complimentary and even more respectful. Eleanor disapproved, believing the change a mistake. No matter. That weekend, Maeve ditched her somber wardrobe and had dressed to impress—namely, herself—ever since.

And in the process became a killer attorney.

For today's important meeting, she'd taken special care with her appearance. In a nod to the cool September weather, she'd paired a meticulously tailored, deep rust-colored one-button blazer with a form-fitting spandex and merino wool designer dress splashed with bold, geometric designs. Her accessories were clunky gold jewelry and a pair of suede high-heeled boots that she'd recently snared at New York's fashion week. They were one of a kind and matched her blazer color exactly. As she drove her pearl-white Aston Martin onto the hallowed grounds of Point du Sable's exclusive country club, she fluffed her curls and glanced in the mirror to check her makeup. Flawless.

"G-g-good morning, Ms. Eddington." The valet rushed to open her door, stumbling over his words as he eyed her appreciatively. "You look...stunning."

"Thank you."

"Whatever perfume you're wearing smells great."

"Thanks." Maeve had already started up the walkway.

"I'll take real good care of your car!" he yelled to her back.

She threw a finger wave over her shoulder, entered the main building and continued down a hallway of private rooms. Plastering her face with a look of bravado that she didn't quite feel, Maeve placed her hand on the knob and took a deep breath. She was walking into a new situation, one that Eddington Enterprise had never handled. The estate-planning department of the financial services company was being sued. For Maeve, losing the case was not an option.

She opened the door, entered the room and locked eyes with the last person on earth she expected to see there— Victor Cortez.

Maeve almost passed out from the shock.

That's how she felt on the inside. On the outside, she pulled her suddenly paralyzed lips into a smile and neared the table of three men now standing to greet her. Purposely ignoring him, she turned to one of two men she'd known would be in attendance.

"Hello, Joel," she greeted, accepting his handshake.

"Good afternoon, Maeve." Joel's expression was one of unabashed admiration. "You're looking lovely as always."

"Thank you." She nodded at the man next to him, before shaking his eagerly outstretched hand. "Patrick."

"Hello, Maeve. It's good to see you."

"Under different circumstances, I'd say the same." A smile revealing perfect white teeth softened the verbal jab. "Where's Cornelius?"

Cornelius Bond was a lifelong Point du Sable (PDS) resident, a longtime friend and associate, and general attorney for the family suing their firm. The attorney she'd expected would be here. Not...*him*.

Joel shifted from one foot to the other. "He, um, has a

full load and feels unable to give this case the attention it deserves. He also has a personal relationship with the clients and doesn't want to present a potential conflict of interest." He nodded at the man who looked even more gorgeous than Maeve remembered. "He's passed the case on to this very capable young man."

He turned toward the man Joel assumed was a stranger. "Victor Cortez. He, too, went to Harvard. Cornelius believed the two of you have met."

"I may have seen him on campus, once or twice."

Maeve steeled herself, and only now allowed her eyes to drift over to the strapping version of alpha-manliness standing close by. Much too close.

"Victor."

Unlike the other two men, Victor didn't quickly rush toward her with his hand out. His eyes slowly roamed her body—seconds, really, when to Maeve it felt like slow motion—before reaching for her hand as though he had every right and bringing it to his full, cushy lips.

"Hello, Maeve."

Yum.

His voice rumbled calm and deep, like the ocean, lightly tinged with the melody of his Caribbean roots. His skin was soft, his grip firm. At five-nine, even without the extra four inches her boots afforded, she looked up into an exquisite face to meet his deep brown eyes. He smelled like power and danger and every woman's fantasy. To not succumb to the sheer magnetism that came with his presence, Maeve would need to stay at the top of her game.

Then the hurt and humiliation still lingering three years after being dumped by her ex—high school sweetheart rose to the surface, a sore—pun intended—reminder that she wasn't on that field anymore.

"It's been a long time."

"Yes, it has."

"Around five years?"

"About that."

"Those years have been good to you. You've done the impossible and gotten even more beautiful than you were at Harvard. Even then you were easily the finest woman around."

Joel chuckled. "Watch out, Maeve. That guy is smoother than an Olympian skating across the ice."

"In that case, some things never change." Said with forced lightness from a woman trying to quell the butterflies circling her stomach and staunch the flow of heat gathering at the apex of her thighs. "Flattery might get you a returned compliment, but it won't help you win this case."

Maeve sat down on unsteady legs. "Gentlemen."

The men sat as well. Now, thankfully, there was a table between her and Victor. Still, his unwavering gaze was like an embrace that she felt to her womanly core. With a focused resolve, she pulled a tablet from her Hermès tote and set it on the table.

"We all know why we're here. To hear the demand on behalf of your clients for this baseless lawsuit."

Victor shifted, his expression appearing to be one of amused confidence as he sat back in his seat. "As you know, by receipt of said demand letter that brought us here," he began without computer or notes, "I am representing the estate of Lillian Agnes Martin Duberry on behalf of beneficiaries Hubert the Third, Agnes and Adele, who are of the belief that not only was their grandmother's sizable investment portfolio mismanaged, but that funds have disappeared from several accounts.

"As the letter states, the children are seeking full and immediate restitution. Because of your family's shared history, and the friendship with the Eddingtons that the Duberrys enjoyed, they are willing to drop any further legal proceedings if those funds are replaced within the next thirty days."

"Funds totaling..." Maeve tapped the tablet's glass and scrolled down. "Approximately ten million dollars, correct?"

"Nine million, six-hundred thirty-two thousand, to be exact."

"How do you do that?" Joel asked, amazed. "Keep all of those facts in your head."

"He's got a big head," Maeve retorted without thinking. "One that size can hold a lot."

"Big head for a big man doing big things," Victor glibly replied, clearly unfazed. "And everyone knows that bigger is better."

The comment was said innocently enough, but Maeve felt all present got the double entendre. She was used to men using subtlety to try to get under her skin.

Victor had done that, big-time, but he'd never know it. To cover the hot naughty thoughts his comment elicited, she lifted a pitcher of lemon-and-mint water from a tray on the table and poured herself a glass.

"Sometimes the greatest gifts come in small packages."

Victor shrugged. "I wouldn't know anything about that."

"Just as our company knows nothing about lost, stolen or otherwise unaccounted for funds due the Duberry heirs. Our staff is highly educated and experienced, their integrity above reproach. The team handling Ms. Duberry's portfolio has assured me of its accuracy. They are pulling together financial records that will be delivered to you along with my response later this week. Once you have those records and speak to your clients, I'm sure they will realize their error and we can quickly put this unfortunate accusation behind us."

"Hopefully they're not the same documents the accountants gave me, listing her holdings at just over three million."

"I'm confident that whatever you have is an accurate reporting, therefore on behalf of Eddington Enterprise, and for the record, I am responding with an unequivocal no to your demand."

"I'm equally sure that once our records have been

viewed by your team that a check in the full amount demanded, and not a pile of paperwork listing random numbers, will be the written response that you provide."

The other men commented but it barely mattered. For Maeve, it seemed Victor was the only one in the room.

There it was then, the conditions of battle. Victor, self-assured. Maeve, confident and unmoving.

For both, regarding the lawsuit, it was clearly game on.

Two

Victor stretched his legs, crossing them at the ankles, as he fingered the card bearing Maeve's name and number. The shock of seeing her had left him, but how good she'd looked and smelled stayed firm on his mind. Since the case involved her family's billion-dollar business, he'd known there was a chance of seeing her while in Point du Sable. But not as opposing counsel. Last he'd heard, she worked for a Chicago law firm. Plus, Cornelius had given Victor another attorney's name, the one he believed handled Eddington Enterprise's litigations and such matters. Maeve entering the small meeting room of the town's luxury country club had taken his breath away. He immediately wanted to be with her. Nothing serious. Long-term was overrated and, according to what he'd personally witnessed, nearly impossible to successfully maintain. But while in the Windy City, Victor thought she could definitely help take the chill off.

Should I call her?

Victor tossed the card on the table, stood and walked to the window, pondering the notion. He was a Four Seasons regular, used to nothing but the best. Looking out of the corner suite's paneless glass, Victor failed to appreciate the panoramic lake and city views. He was back at Harvard, with Cornelius, asking about the leggy beauty who'd just walked in the room.

* * *

"Who's that?" For the first time that night since being roped into attending a friend's birthday party, Victor's interest in the attendees was piqued.

"Who?" Cornelius asked, over the thumping bass of a hip-hop favorite.

Victor nodded toward the door.

"Oh, her. That's Maeve Eddington. Strictly off-limits."

This comment garnered a raised brow as his eyes drank her in. The high ponytail. Skinny jeans. Off-the-shoulder mohair sweater. Heeled thigh-high boots.

His dick twitched, signaling the desire for an up close meet-and-greet. Victor was totally in agreement with said body part. To say the woman was attractive would be akin to an insult. Her beauty was in a whole other category, different stratosphere.

"Her brother, Desmond, was a big shot at Columbia, business wunderkind. He's now working alongside their father, Derrick, at Eddington Enterprise, one of the most successful financial services companies in the world. Both Society members. Power. Influence. With both Maeve and her equally stunning sister, Reign, the rule is look but don't touch."

Victor barely heard Cornelius's warning. His legs had started moving in Maeve's direction of their own accord.

And then he was beside her. "Hello, gorgeous."

She turned mesmerizing brown eyes with gold flecks in his direction. Gave him the once-over. "Hi."

"Name's Victor." He held out a hand. She shook it. "Victor Cortez."

"Oh, you're that Victor."

"Uh-oh. What does that mean?"

"I've heard about you. You were engaged to Felicity Noble, cheated on her and broke her heart."

Victor wasn't surprised that she'd heard the story. His ex had told everyone but *TMZ* her version of what happened to cause the breakup, a story that bore little resemblance to the truth. Victor allowed the moment designed to help his ex save face. Family and true friends knew the real score. That's all that mattered. Victor didn't need to convince a campus otherwise, didn't feel the need to put on a good-guy campaign. Those who wanted to believe the worst, so be it. Victor Cortez didn't suffer from low self-esteem.

"Can't believe everything you hear," he finally answered.

Maeve cocked her head to the side. "So you're not a lying, cheating playboy?"

"Not last time I checked, though I admit to being guilty of enjoying a mutually agreed upon good time."

"Ah, a good time. That's what you called it. Among committed parties, the more common word used is *affair*."

"Between her and I, the most commonly used word now is *over*." He held up his glass. "Can I get you a drink?"

Her eyes narrowed, the chin raised slightly beneath a pair of sinfully full lips. "No, thank you, Victor Cortez."

She blessed him with a catlike smile before melding into the crowd of partygoers. He found himself searching for her, his thoughts drawn to her, for the rest of the night. He told himself it was because of her disinterest. Victor loved nothing more than a good challenge. But even as he tried to convince himself of this angle, he knew the way his heart palpitated when he saw her was different than his reaction toward other beautiful women. Maeve Eddington—there was something about her.

Later, he learned from Cornelius that while Victor was in his last year at Harvard Law School, this was her first. As his friend went on about her, he noticed something else. Cornelius was sprung. Besotted. Beyond infatuated. Cornelius denied it, said that to him Maeve was more like a sister. Their families had known each other all of their lives. Victor didn't believe a word of it, but didn't argue. In his mind, Cornelius's loss was every other man's gain.

Not that it mattered. Other than in a hallway, on the

school grounds or at a party here and there, he barely saw Maeve. He graduated, returned to set up residences in both his hometown, Puerto Limon, and the country's capital, San Jose, and began assisting in the governing of Costa Rica, alongside his high-profile father. Days were long. Nights were short. Women were plentiful. Soon enough, thoughts about Maeve Eddington slipped from Victor's mind. But he never forgot her.

Victor grabbed his phone from a counter, returned to the table and picked up the business card. His heartbeat increased as he punched in her number and listened to the rings.

She's probably busy or screening her calls.

Victor was sure the call would go to voice mail and began mentally preparing the message he'd leave when—

"Hello?"

Her voice was low and slightly raspy. It brought to mind the sweetness of sticky molasses poured on top of a sensual summer breeze.

"Maeve, hey. It's Victor."

"Hello, Victor. What's up?"

"Nothing official or too serious. We didn't have the chance earlier for a real conversation. I called to invite you out to dinner so that we can catch up."

There was a long pause during which the unthinkable happened. Victor caught a case of nerves, something he hadn't experienced since his fourth-grade self summoned up the courage to ask his pretty neighbor Bonita out to a Halloween party.

"Thanks, Victor, but I must decline the offer. My family's close relationship and long history with the Duberrys already makes this a sensitive case. Considering our adversarial positions, I don't think that's wise."

"You do know it's possible to not mix business with pleasure."

"I don't view as pleasurable socializing with the legal counsel bringing a lawsuit against my firm."

"There are dozens of other things we can discuss besides that."

"Such as…"

"Life. Current affairs. What you've been doing since I last saw you all those years ago."

"That's a quick conversation. I've been working. Running a company's legal department leaves little time for anything else."

"No boyfriend, fiancé, husband, children?"

"None of the above."

"One of those career women driven to topple all men off the corporate ladder and secure the top rung."

"I strive to be the best of what I do and knock off all opponents, no matter the gender."

"A real man-eater," Victor drawled. "I should have known."

"Look, I'd love to chitchat, but my workday is not over."

"Are you preparing a response to my demand letter? Let me save you some time, darling. Have your company write the check."

"I'm not your darling, *sweetie*." Condescension dripped between each consonant and vowel.

"I meant no offense. Didn't know you were one of those."

"Those who?"

"Women who feel that to make it in a man's world, they have to stop being a woman. Women who don't realize that in actuality the world belongs to them."

"What if this conversation was with Joel or Patrick? Would you use that endearment in reference to them?"

"That would be a negative…counselor. For either of those two, it would more likely be *asshole*, *chump* or *dweeb*."

She chuckled, proving he'd lightened the mood as intended. "*Chump*? I think my grandfather is the last person I heard use that word."

"You've got a cool grandpops."

"I do, indeed. And for the record, you have no idea who I am."

A brief, comfortable silence settled between them. When Victor spoke, his words were wrapped in kindness.

"I have the utmost respect for you, Maeve, and for your family. I've read up on Eddington Enterprise. The company's making big moves. The innovative software that's changing how banks and other financial institutions do business. Your foray into digital currency with the offering E-Squared. The hype was so powerful I bought a block. So far, it's been a worthwhile investment.

"I guess what I'm saying is we can cut through the chase and save us both time and money. A company as successful as yours probably has what we're asking for in petty cash."

"As stated during our earlier meeting, you'll soon receive a more detailed report documenting our response. Until then, take care, Victor."

"Until next time."

Victor walked into the suite's bedroom and pulled workout clothes from his luggage. Speaking with Maeve stirred up all kinds of pent-up energy. Since he wasn't into spending time with random women, a jog by the lake would have to suffice as a means to release it.

Five miles, and still he was unable to outrun his thoughts of Maeve. Back in the suite, under a steaming hot shower, mental pictures of her at the meeting taunted him still—her long curly hair, expressive eyes, kissable lips and legs that went on forever.

Crazy to have that kind of effect on him after one short meeting. As much as that bugged him, Victor knew one thing for sure—he couldn't wait to see her again.

Three

"My goodness, sister, this man is gorgeous!"

Maeve looked over at her sister, Reign, who was checking out online pictures of Victor while sprawled across her king-size four-poster bed.

"I told you he was attractive."

"Dad's attractive. Michael B. Jordan is attractive. Regé-Jean Page is super attractive. But this guy... I mean, like... wow."

"Okay, Reign, be careful. Sounds like you're about to drool on my spread."

"Hey, I'm just saying." She clicked on and enlarged another picture. "Is he as tall as he looks?"

"Around six-four, six-five, I'd imagine. A giant compared to your petite five foot four."

"Tall, dark and heart-attack handsome. All business protocol and rivalry aside, Maeve, I wouldn't let this one get away."

"I'm not interested." *Much.* Maeve trounced into a walk-in closet the size of most bedrooms. "Besides, he lives in another country. We had a couple mutual friends in college but since then have traveled in different circles. Our paths haven't crossed before now in over five years. Once this case is over, it will likely be another five."

Or fifteen. Or forever. That prospect did not feel good.

"Where's he from?"

"I think he was born somewhere in the Caribbean. But if

not raised in the States, he spent a lot of time here, including all eight or so years it took for him to get his Juris Doctorate."

"At Harvard with you, right?"

"Same school. Different crowd."

"Do you think he'll be at the party tonight?"

"I don't know."

But she'd considered it, which is why a small mountain of designer originals was now heaped on the floor. The party being held at the country club was a birthday celebration for Dalia, Cornelius's sister. Victor being in town on behalf of Cornelius, along with their shared college experience and past friendship, made it likely for him to appear on the guest list. Maeve told herself that whether or not he showed up didn't matter, that she didn't want to see him, anyway.

But it did matter. And she wanted to see him. End of story. Bottom line.

"What about this?"

Maeve held up a cranberry-colored, wide-legged jumpsuit, with a cinched belt collar and plunging V-neck.

"It's cute but…" Reign climbed off the bed and joined Maeve in the dressing room. "You want to wear something that will make a statement. If he's there, you'll want to stand out as though you're the only woman in the room."

"He, who?"

Reign laughed. "Try that with someone who hasn't known you her entire life. You've never taken this much time to choose an outfit."

She walked over to a row of gowns, flipped through them and landed on one near the back. "Try on this one."

Maeve looked at a dress she'd purchased on an international shopping spree and at the dare of a friend. It was spectacular. Black, formfitting, with a spray of crystals going from shoulder to hem. Plunging back. Split exposing almost an entire right leg. The dress with a bodice of mesh and lace was designed to fit a woman's body like a second skin, but in a material that provided respectability by being non-clingy.

"You don't think that's over-the-top?"

Reign gave her a look. "Is there anything too dressy for our crowd, or the club?"

"You've got a point."

"Then it's settled. This dress." Reign crossed over to a wall covered with a cubby-holed fixture holding shoes. "And these heels. Keep your jewelry simple. The dress is enough. Let me know if it works for a proper seduction," she teased as she left the room.

"Where are you going?"

"To get ready, sister. You're not the only princess attending the ball."

Reign dressed quickly and looked fabulous in a silver super mini that highlighted her hourglass frame. She returned to the home Maeve had built a year ago, less than a mile from the family's main mansion, and helped to ensure her sister's look was complete. Maeve's thick long curls were piled high atop her head, with errant tendrils left draping her face. She kept makeup minimal—foundation, powder, mascara and gloss.

Once finished, Reign stepped back in appraisal of her masterpiece. "You look amazing, Maeve."

"Thanks, Reign. You've always been more fashionable than me."

"You got all the smarts. I had to do something."

"Stop it with that. You can do anything."

"Anything within the Eddington idea of achievement. Not anything I want."

Maeve wisely chose to stay silent. Reign had been fighting with their parents for more than a year over her desire to ditch her corporate career for an around-the-world adventure as an influencer with a travel video blog, financed by that "idea of achievement" Reign seemed to eschew.

"You want to ride over together?"

Reign shook her head. "Paul's coming by to get me."

Maeve checked her watch. "Then I guess I'll head over. See you later?"

"Absolutely. Unless you get swept off your feet and whisked away from the party."

"That has zero chance of happening. I'll see you there."

The ballroom had been transformed into a fall fantasy. Colorful silk leaves dotted with crystals that swayed in the air above them on near-invisible strings, creating a fantastical oasis. The ceiling had been draped in gold chiffon, matching the gold leaf sprayed on life-sized ice carvings of the birthday girl Dalia's favorite celebrities. The music was loud and current. The food, delectable. The drink, nonstop. Maeve easily navigated the familiar crowd, making small talk with the circle of people she'd known since they all were children.

"May I have this dance?"

She'd almost forgotten about Victor, until his voice poured into her ear like molten lava from an active volcano. She braced herself, then turned to face him as the sounds of a slow R&B number with a steady bass beat swirled around them.

"Sure you can handle that?" she asked to cover her own lack of confidence in actually being up for the job.

"I'll take my chances."

He reached for her hand, which was quickly enveloped in his much larger one. They stepped onto the already crowded dance floor. He pulled her to him, his manner sure, authoritative, then wrapped his strong, toned arms around her and set up a sensual sway.

"I was hoping to see you tonight," he whispered, his hot, damp breath causing her skin to tingle.

"Really? Why?"

"You're my favorite sparring partner."

His answer was as shocking as it was unexpected. Most of Maeve's dates were intimidated by her intellect and verbal ability. Here, this guy was acting like such traits were a bonus. He threw her off-kilter. She didn't like that at all.

"You consider that civil conversation we had during our meeting a fight?"

"No, but I saw enough of your fire to know you can

bring it. For me, that doesn't happen often. I welcome the challenge."

The song soared to its crescendo. Victor tightened his grip. He smelled good. Looked good. Felt even better. Everything about the man was driving her crazy. Maeve held onto his broad shoulders and her sanity, although with the latter she was less successful than she'd hoped. All she could think about was how long it had been since her last intimate encounter, and how thoroughly she was certain Victor could meet her every erotic demand and supply every need. The song ended. His arms fell away. She felt abandoned. Her body thrummed, hungry with desire. She hid the tumult of rampant emotions behind a casual smile.

"You've got moves, I see," she joked.

"Trust me, darling, you haven't seen anything yet."

They parted and for the rest of the night Maeve did what she could to avoid him. His body, though, was like a GPS signal. She could sense his presence when he neared her, could feel his gaze on her skin. At one point in the evening, she found a bistro table in the corner, partially hidden by a wall and tall potted plants. She watched Victor easily command the space around him, saw women fairly swoon when they entered his realm. She rolled her eyes. Clearly, this was not her situation. Even if she fancied a playboy, which she did not, she wouldn't choose someone garnering such fierce competition that fighting off her detractors would be a full-time job. In the lingo of football, one of her favorite sports, dating someone like Victor would surely be an "L" situation. Better to stay focused on business, the boardroom and the lawsuit, where instead of losing something major, like the case, or her heart, she was sure to pull off a win.

Four

Victor sat at the dining room table of his luxury suite, poring over the mountain of information he'd requested regarding the Duberry case, and the documents included in Maeve's begrudgingly impressive and thorough initial response. From the evidence he'd been presented with, something clearly did not add up. As thorough as the paperwork seemed, and as upstanding a citizen as Hubert and the sisters appeared, Victor had gotten "a feeling" from the moment they met, shortly after agreeing to take over the case from Cornelius. He couldn't put his finger on what was bothering him about the facts as he knew them, nor could he find a hole in what she'd presented.

Part of the magic that made Victor such a successful businessman—he never ignored "a feeling."

At his first detailed glance, all the documentation appeared legitimate. Bank statements. Financial records. Decades of meticulous accounting captured in a series of color-coded spreadsheets. Verified records obtained through subpoena. One clear bottom line was drawn as the wedge between them. One called account balances. Dinero. Money. And why almost ten million dollars of what the estate documents reports to have had was unaccounted for.

Whose paperwork was right, Eddington Enterprise or that gathered by the trustees of the Duberry estate? Was the amount from the Duberry accounts accurate and if so, what happened? Was it stolen? Lost? Spent? Was there an account sitting in a stock balance or mutual fund that had yet to be uncovered? Those were questions both Victor and Maeve wanted answered, the sooner the better for all parties involved.

He spun his executive chair around, got up and walked to the window that looked out on Lake Michigan. Island guys were always drawn to the water. It was in their blood. Gazing out on the tranquil blue massive lake calmed him, allowed him to think more clearly. To replay his interaction with Maeve with an unattached, critical eye. Yes, there was an attraction, a magnetism between them. It had always been there, weaving a web around the handful of times they'd socialized. But he'd never seriously considered the possibility of their getting together romantically. There was an aura around Maeve that bore an exclusivity, a natural uniqueness without trying that set her apart from the rest. Their families were equally wealthy, yet Maeve had still always felt above his pay grade. Only now, in the boardroom over a legal situation, did he feel the playing field level. When it came to law, he was well on his way to becoming a GOAT, one of the greatest attorneys of all time. To be the best, above all the rest, you could only play to win.

His cell phone buzzed. He thought of Maeve and checked the ID. That it wasn't her shouldn't have bothered him as much as it did.

"What's up, Cornelius?" He pressed the speaker button, placed the phone on the counter and poured sparkling water into a glass.

"That's what I called to find out. We didn't get a chance to talk at Dalia's party. How was the briefing?"

"Interesting. Maeve Eddington is handling the case."

"Really? I'm surprised."

"Me, too. I thought she worked here in Chicago."

"She did until a few years ago. Honed her chops while steadily climbing the ranks. Could have made partner had she chosen to stay there. She's good, Victor. Don't under-estimate her."

"I won't. She turned down the demand, which is what I expected."

"I told you that more than likely this would go to trial. Damned shame, considering the history. Lillian was one of Derrick's first customers. Her patronage helped to le-gitimize him. Her referrals resulted in dozens of wealthy clients. They should agree to a quick resolution through full restitution based on that alone. Honor her memory, for God's sake."

"Even if it turned out the money was transferred out of their possession, as their records indicate?"

"I don't believe that's possible, but to not drag Lillian's name through the rumor mill mud, yes, even then."

A feeling stirred in Victor's gut. "Did you and Maeve ever date?"

"Where'd that come from?"

"From wanting to know the answer."

"My defense of the Duberry family has nothing to do with Maeve, or the Eddingtons. It's not personal. As I explained when I requested your representation on their behalf, all of our families know each other, and mine and the Duberry family are close friends. A clear conflict of interest."

Two chances to answer and both times deflected. Vic-tor stored that tidbit away in his photographic memory.

"You know, in full disclosure, perhaps I do have a bit of a personal investment. The siblings' father, Hubert Jr., was like a big brother to me. I felt I owed finding them the best attorney that money could buy. Outside of my-self, that is you."

"My brother!" Victor appreciated Cornelius's rare show of bold confidence.

"No doubt." Cornelius cleared his throat. "Hubert strug-gled under the weight of his grandfather's legacy and his fa-ther's success. Hubert the Third now feels the weight of that mantle. The twins, Agnes and Adele, are working to shine while in the shadow of their society grandmother, one that is cast far and wide. Agnes has gone the educational route and will probably marry well. Adele is rebellious and has tried to forge a path outside of high society. But all of them loved their grandmother. I'm sure they are only trying to preserve what the family established."

Victor remained silent, absorbing not only Cornelius's words but the emotion behind them.

There was silence on both ends before Cornelius added, "Maeve and I went out, but never dated."

But you wanted to, was the mental comeback Victor kept to himself.

"You're already a respected, well-known successful attorney in your own right and don't need any help from me. But a successful representation of someone as revered as Lillian Duberry, in a place like Point du Sable with tentacles into money and power all over the world, will be a feather in your legal cap for sure."

"You're spot on, Cornelius, my man. I don't need any help from you."

The call ended. Victor checked his watch. Time passed quickly these days but with his limited contacts in the area, and predilection for whom he wanted to be around, he still had too much of it on his hands. Against his better judgment and previous declarations, he found himself calling Maeve. One word, her hello, put him in a better mood.

"What time is dinner?"

"Whatever time you order room service or secure a restaurant table."

"You are some kind of woman."

"Victor, what do you want?"

"To spend time with you, for old times' sake."

"What old times are you talking about? We never spent time together."

"Then it's a situation that's long past due. Do you have dinner plans?"

"Actually, I do."

"I'm not surprised. What about tomorrow?"

"Brunch with the family, standing reservation."

"Any room for guests?"

"Didn't I already explain why it wouldn't be wise for us to socialize? We are working on opposite sides of a lawsuit."

"We attended Harvard together."

"I barely knew you."

"You knew me."

"I knew *of* you. There's a difference."

"Are you telling me that I'm not welcome at this family brunch? Where I'm from, even strangers get invited to Sunday dinner, especially ones who are in a big city like Chicago all by his lonesome."

"You need to pull out that global list of potentials I'm sure you've compiled since college and see if one of them in or near this area wants company."

"Wow, that's cold."

"This is Chicago. Wind blows like that." She huffed. He swore he could feel the chill through the phone. "Isn't Cornelius back in town? Why don't you spend time with his family? Unlike you and I, who barely knew each other, the two of you are good friends."

"I'm not asking Cornelius for his hospitality." Victor continued, overemphasizing his lilting accent. "This tired, frustrated soul, far from home and devoid of local family, is kindly asking if any compassion can be found in your heart to spare him a meal."

"Is this some kind of ploy to get on my good side?"

She sounded gruff and irritated but Victor heard the smile in her voice.

"It is a sincere request for good company and great food."

A second passed. And then another. And then a few more.

"There will be plenty of other guests there besides yourself. Mingle with them. Don't expect me to babysit you."

"Thank you most kindly." That got him an unladylike snort. "What time should I arrive?"

"First pour is at eleven. I'll text the address."

"I look forward to seeing you then."

The call ended without her bothering to reply. She'd tried to appear unflappable, but he'd gotten under her skin. That whole feeling thing and all. He was sure of it.

He mentally replayed the conversation and chuckled. Maeve Eddington was one tough cookie. Victor wasn't worried. He loved sweets.

Five

So great and extensive was the security at the Estates, that most front doors were always unlocked. Such was the case Sunday morning when Maeve opted for fresh air over convenience and walked the short distance to her parents' hilltop mansion. She greeted Chauncey, the butler and house manager, who was busy dusting an already spotless picture frame.

"Mom in the garden?"

"Of course." He stopped dusting as she passed. "You look exceptionally lovely."

"Thanks, Chauncey."

"Is there a new beau joining us today?"

Maeve stopped so quickly she almost tripped on the air beneath her foot. "Why would you say that?"

Chauncey's face became a mask of neutrality. "No reason, my darling."

"*I'm not your darling*," Maeve hastily retorted, as Victor's teasing smile instantly flashed in her mind. If Chauncey used that endearment once, he'd used it a hundred times. Being reminded of Victor was the only reason it rankled. That the arrogant attorney never seemed far from her thoughts annoyed her even more.

Feeling badly, she looped an arm around the butler's shoulders. "I'm sorry for snapping. You're a sweetheart."

Chauncey shook his head. "Just a doddering old man

long past his prime and out of chances, ready to live vicariously through the lucky man who gains your hand."

"Does your wife know about this *past your prime* business?"

"Are you kidding? She's the one who informed me."

"News to you, huh?"

"I had no idea!"

Laughing together and once more back in the good graces of a man more like an uncle than staff, Maeve continued down the long wide hall boasting priceless art, through several rooms and down a small flight of stairs to the solarium, better known as Mona's inside garden. Her mother was standing near the head table, speaking with Chauncey's wife, Bernice, and John, the head chef. Maeve plucked a strawberry from an artistic fruit arrangement on her way to joining the group.

Bernice was the first to greet her. "My, don't we look fancy!"

"What do you mean? I look the same as always. Hi, John." She kissed Mona's cheek. "Hi, Mom."

"Hey, yourself. I agree with Bernice. You put an extra oomph into that outfit. Is it new?"

"This old thing?" That she'd just pulled the tags from. "I've had it forever." A whopping twenty-four hours.

Mona gave her a look that telegraphed, *Mother knows better*, before resuming her conversation with John. "I appreciate your thinking about expanding the dessert table. It's a good idea. In addition to the regular confections let's give a nod to the fall season by adding—" she looked down at the note card he'd given her "—the chai-spiced pumpkin cupcakes, tri-berry cobbler, pear tart and the caramel-pecan cheesecake pie."

Maeve's eyes widened as she watched John leave the room. "Is there going to be a treadmill by each table for use after the meal?"

Mona chuckled. "No, but the indoor sports court is open

and heated, and, if preferred, there are eighteen pristine holes for walking just down the lane."

"Who are today's guests?"

"Cayden's mom, Tami, though she's now more like family."

Maeve nodded. Cayden was her brother Jake's longtime best friend, who'd become an unofficial member of the family and an invaluable asset to Eddington Enterprise.

"Bob Masters RSVP'd. He's still getting over the unexpected loss of his wife. I thought a little socializing might help and am glad he responded."

"Yes, socializing mixed with a little Mona matchmaking."

"Who, *moi*?" Mona placed a hand to her heart. "That the two happen to be seated next to each other is pure coincidence."

Maeve pursed her lips, listening as Mona reeled off several more names. "And Cornelius," she finished.

"Cornelius Bond?"

Mona gave her a look. "You have a problem with that?"

She shouldn't have. Sure, he was the Duberry's family attorney, a fact her mother probably knew since her parents shared everything, but he wasn't handling the lawsuit against the Eddington firm. No, the guy *she'd* invited was in charge of that.

"No problem," she said at last. "I'm just surprised, that's all. Can't remember him joining us in a while."

"Yes, well it seems he and Desmond ran into each other recently at the club. They got talking and Desmond told him he was welcome to stop by."

"Have you finished the seating arrangements?" Maeve picked up a card nearest her as she tried to sound as casual as possible.

"Just finishing up. Why?"

"Because I have a late addition, Victor Cortez. He's... we're...working a case."

Only now did Maeve realize that what she'd already thought of as a very bad idea was actually infinitely worse than that. She'd been roped into inviting to dinner the man helping to sue her family! What had she been thinking or drinking or both?

"Is he the reason behind that dress to impress?"

"Mom, I strive to always look impressive. Just as you taught me."

"Well, you look especially impressive today." Her mother picked up a calligraphy pen and wrote his name on a blank linen card. She looked across the table. "I'll move Tami and Bob to our table so the two of you can sit together."

"No need to do that, Mom. He and I go back to my college days and will have time to visit before he leaves town. *Most likely in a courtroom.* The point of Victor coming here is to mix and mingle with the folk of Point du Sable. Also, he knows Cornelius. Seating them together would be a good idea."

"Hmm, okay."

Maeve could almost see the wheels turning in her mother's mind and was grateful when the servers came in and began setting the tables.

Mona looked around, running a hand through her new short cut. "I'm going to freshen up and make sure Derrick doesn't need anything."

"Sounds good. I'm going to check in on Reign."

On her way to the wing Reign had taken over once Maeve had had her home built and moved out, she sent a group text to her brothers. They needed a heads-up that opposing counsel would soon be in the building.

FYI, Victor Cortez will be at brunch today.

Jake's response was immediate. WTH?

Five minutes later, Desmond chimed in. Sleeping with the enemy? Don't even think about it!

Maeve's eyes widened at her brother's assumption, which for better or worse was spot on. Having hot and heavy sex with Victor Cortez had crossed her mind more than once.

Are you kidding? I'm thinking strategy, not sleepovers.

Maeve thought that white lie sounded so good it deserved serious consideration.

What are you trying to win? A lawsuit or a lawyer? :)

Someone must have told Jake that he was a comedian. Before Maeve could respond, Desmond added his two cents. Good question, bro!

Maeve fired back with a middle finger emoji.

Reign answered Maeve's tap on the double French doors. "Come on in, sis. What's up?"

"You don't want to know," Maeve responded, before providing the Victor update.

An hour later, almost every seat at each table in the solarium was occupied. A pianist sat at a collection of keyboards, providing the diners with a jazzy backdrop. A murmur of conversations rose above the clanking of silver and the ringing of crystal. Maeve sat at the main table, which was next to one for special guests. She worked to appear engaged in conversation with Cayden's wife, Avery, who'd bounced back into her event-planning business after time away to become a new mom, and had recently been recognized by Chicago's Chamber of Commerce.

"Cayden wants me to turn over the entire operation to the office manager and be a full-time mom." She used air quotes.

"What did you tell him?"

"That all moms are full-time. Whether at home or at work, we never stop being parents, right?"

Maeve nodded, überaware of when Trinity Taylor, the beautiful daughter of her dad's classmate just back from an internship in Europe, tossed her curls in laughter and placed her hand on Victor's arm.

"But helping to bring people's birthdays, weddings and other milestone events to life isn't just a job, but my passion. Know what I mean?"

"Um, yes, I do." She forced her gaze from the peripheral view of Victor, whose quiet yet animated exchange commanded the attention of everyone at the table, and focused fully on Avery.

Maeve admired Avery. She appreciated the chance to spend more time with her. When speaking, her words were sincere.

"You're not only skilled but gifted at what you do. Being able to spend time doing what you love probably makes you a better mom."

"My thoughts, exactly. Later on, will you please convey them to my husband?"

Maeve smiled as she took a sip of mimosa. "I'll see what I can do."

The entrée service ended. Guests stood and mingled while having their plates cleared and awaiting dessert. Other than a casual greeting when he arrived, and introductions to her less-than-enthusiastic brothers and her sister, Reign, she and Victor hadn't spoken. Yet, a spotlight couldn't have made him stand out more in the room. He was meticulously groomed and wore a cream-colored turtleneck with black slacks and loafers, looking more handsome in casual wear than he did in a suit. Maeve figured the afternoon would be spent avoiding his advances. He didn't approach her. Nor did he lack for undivided attention, more often than not of the female variety. The script had been flipped without her knowledge, and definitely without her consent. Instead of Victor chasing her skirt tails, she felt like the hunter trying to capture the prey. Not a minute had passed, even a second perhaps, when she hadn't been aware of Victor's presence. It was almost as if an aura of magnetic electricity existed around him, one that drew her in and others as well. Once or twice, she felt his eyes on her, and physically reacted. Her skin tingled, remembering the feel of his body when they'd danced, and the expert touch of his big strong hands. He smiled and her imagination brought his lips to her own. She could almost smell his cologne. His gaze, though brief and friendly, felt seductive, searing through her clothing and into her soul.

The brunch had gone exactly as planned. He'd left her alone, made friends with others as she'd so curtly suggested. It took effort for her not to pout as a favorite saying of her grandmother's came to mind.

Be careful what you ask for. You might get it.

Six

For the entirety of the brunch, Victor was aware of Maeve. Who she talked to, where she walked, almost when she moved. He'd always been a socializer, never met a stranger and easily conversed with the guests at the table, including Cornelius and his date, who arrived early in the festivities. During each painful moment of the elaborate yet deftly casual two-hour affair, it took every ounce of restraint and discipline, traits he thought he had in spades, to stay away from her. She looked, in a word, *delicious*. The sweater dress fit like a glove he wished was on his hand, its off-the-shoulder design emphasizing the long neck he could imagine covering with kisses and highlighting the rich brown skin he'd bet was smoother than silk. The color reminded him of a caramel candy he'd loved in childhood, a taffy-like bar of gooey sweetness that he'd unwrap with giddy anticipation, then slowly lick, suck and savor down to the last bite. The same as he'd do to her, if given the chance.

If, or when?

"Surprised to see you here."

Slightly annoyed at the interruption of his fantasy, Victor shifted to see who'd spoken. *Ah, Maeve's brother.*

"Desmond, correct?"

"That's right."

"I recently scrolled your accomplishments online. You're doing big things!"

"Speaking of big things, my brother and I have been

wondering something all afternoon. Where did you hide the crane?"

"Crane," Victor repeated with furrowed brow.

"Yes. Someone with balls big enough to invite himself to the home owned by the company he's suing must use some type of contraption to carry them around."

Victor's smile was genuine. He liked this guy.

"A bit of extra courage perhaps, but no crane."

Desmond crossed his arms, his stance challenging, authoritative. "What's your angle?"

Victor's posture remained relaxed, his voice as calm as the eye in a Category Five. "Regarding the lawsuit? No angle and nothing personal, just a search for the truth."

"I was speaking about my sister."

"What about me?"

At the sound of her voice, Victor's heart skittered around in his chest. He was immediately aware of the cologne she wore, the same as when he'd held her in his arms at the party and could have danced the night away.

"I was about to inform him that professionally you were unbeatable and personally you were off-limits."

"Thanks, brother, but in both areas, I can handle Victor."

Victor's smile spread as slowly as melted butter on toast. "Is that right?"

"Easily." Maeve gave him a bold once-over that telegraphed her not being a pushover.

His smile broadened as he nodded. "I've been duly warned."

Victor looked beyond her shoulder. Cornelius and his date strode toward them and once there, addressed the group.

"Hello, everyone." After various responses, he continued, "Desmond has already had the pleasure but Maeve, Victor, this is Peyton Hall. She's from Lansing, Michigan, here visiting her cousins, the Sherwoods, and entertaining the idea of moving here to the Point."

"Yolanda is your cousin?" Maeve asked the petite woman whose cute face reminded her of a young Janet Jackson.

"Yes" was the soft-spoken response.

"She and my sister, Reign, graduated high school together." Maeve searched the room for her sister, before turning back to Peyton. "Did you get a chance to meet her?"

Peyton shook her head.

"Reign left a while ago," Desmond told her. "Before the entrée, I think."

The siblings telegraphed a look between them that Victor couldn't decipher. Much easier to read was the barely veiled look of interest in the surreptitious glances Peyton threw his way.

"I'll tell my sister you're visiting," Maeve continued. "She goes everywhere and knows everybody. Maybe you, her and Yolanda should spend a night out."

"That would be nice." Peyton looked at Victor. "Did I detect an accent earlier when you spoke?"

"Caribbean, by way of Costa Rica."

"I thought that was Central America," Peyton responded, clearly confused.

"It is, but my grandparents are Jamaican, as were the majority of residents who first settled Puerto Limon."

"I've always wanted to visit Costa Rica," Peyton continued, coming out of her shell while speaking to Victor. I have a friend who attended a wedding in a place called Uvita. She said it was like being in paradise."

As Victor responded, he noticed two things—Maeve trying to act uninterested and Cornelius trying to hide his displeasure.

"Uvita and my hometown are equally beautiful, and on almost the exact opposite sides of the country."

"You're here on business?"

Cornelius's annoyance grew. Victor looked from his college friend to Maeve's sparkling eyes and realized he wasn't the only one who'd made the observation. He worked to not laugh out loud.

"Yes, working with Cornelius as a matter of fact."

"Oh!" She looked from him to Cornelius and back. "What do you—"

"My, look at the time," Cornelius interrupted, faux-checking his watch. "Peyton, we should get moving. The matinee we're attending has a private reception beforehand with the director and actors. We don't want to be late."

He placed a possessive arm around Peyton and whisked her away so fast the group's goodbyes were said to the couple's backs. They all watched as Cornelius slowed near the solarium's outside entrance only long enough to shake Derrick's and Mona's hands. Victor looked at Maeve, who looked from him to Desmond, who looked at them both, before they all dissolved into quiet chuckles.

Desmond spoke to Victor without menace for the first time since meeting. "Bro, I guess she was showing you a little too much interest."

"You think?" Maeve asked.

"Come on, guys. The young lady was interested in my beautiful country, as are many who find out I'm from there."

"Yeah, okay," Desmond said, his look serious once again. "And if you believe that, I've got some oceanfront land for sale here in the Midwest."

Maeve cast an eye at her brother, before focusing on Victor. "And I've got a yacht that you can sail on that ocean."

The group enjoyed another laugh. Victor watched Maeve look across the room and wave at a guest. He turned in the direction of her interest and saw a guy who, during the course of dinner, he felt had spent way too much time with his woman.

His woman? Where had that come from?

No matter, it's how he felt. There was no misogyny intended in his heart over the notion that Maeve belonged to him. He immediately felt some kind of way about the forty-something-looking gentleman in a tailored suit with matching shirt and tie, smiling at Maeve as though he'd just won the lottery. The thought to march over and punch the guy out totally crossed his mind. Instead, he maintained his cool, deciding to take the upper hand in their parting.

"It seems as though your parents may be leaving," he began, just before Maeve was set to open her mouth and announce her betrayal to leave him for Mr. Matching. "I want to let them know how much I appreciate their hospitality, and what an awesome job they've done in raising such a fine family, and such a well-rounded, accommodating daughter." He shook Desmond's hand, and kissed his wife Ivy's cheek.

Then he turned to Maeve.

"Thanks for the invite, love," he huskily murmured, placing a whispery kiss at her temple as he massaged the tender part of her wrist with his thumb. "The food was delicious, the company entertaining." He stepped back to look her in her eye. "And you've never looked more beautiful."

"It's what I would have done for anyone," she answered as though nonplussed.

Victor's smile was cocky. The racing pulse he'd run his thumb over told an entirely different story. Driving home in his rented luxury car, his mind whirled. He had a lot to think about. There was no denying the magic that swirled around him and Maeve. But seeing her in her familial environment had given him pause. Clearly, her family was close-knit. Her parents seemed to enjoy a loving, successful marriage. Growing up, he hadn't known what that looked like. His father, dashing, extroverted and in demand both professionally and personally, had often succumbed to outside attractions, which led to his parents divorcing when he was thirteen. His mother was understandably bitter. She unknowingly drove into his mind that there was no way a man could be faithful. That marriage wasn't something to be desired, only endured. During his dad's second wedded union, Victor left home and went off to college. By the time the senior Cortez finally outgrew the penchant for skirt chasing and married wife number three, Victor's view of marriage had already been formed. By and large, they didn't work. He'd never gotten to see what a successful union looked like, not up close and personal anyway. This was why he'd always imagined himself as a life-long bachelor or one of those stereotypical old men who, once in their fifties or sixties and past their prime, decided to settle down and have a family with some young thing half his age.

Then, almost on a whim and out of boredom from his somewhat predictable life, he'd taken on a case for an old college buddy and crossed paths with the beautiful, seemingly unavailable Maeve Eddington. Her reentry into his life had him rethinking his bachelor plans.

When he'd returned to Costa Rica, it was with the intent of building a life there, making his homeland or somewhere in the country nearby his permanent residence. But maybe Peyton had it right. Maybe Point du Sable was a destination to be considered. It wouldn't be the first time Victor had uprooted his life and lived across continents. He thought he'd never do it again. But Maeve, with that ridiculously hot body and formidable mind, was giving a very strong reason to reconsider.

Seven

"I don't like him." Desmond aimed a striped pool ball into the table's right corner slot, and missed.

It was the Saturday following the brunch Victor had attended and the first opportunity her siblings had to grill Maeve on what they thought had been a questionable decision—inviting an opponent onto their home turf. In the days that had followed that dinner, Desmond and Cayden, the siblings' brother from another mother, had handled business out of town. Jake had been knee-deep in managing the extensive portfolio of the country's newest superstar pro athlete. Reign was busy being Reign—flapping her social butterfly wings as the company's public relations director while dating her latest celebrity heartthrob. Today, though, was a rare moment when they had the mansion to themselves, with Desmond and Maeve traipsing up to the main house where Jake and Reign still lived. With Derrick and Mona on an impromptu trip to the Bahamas and Desmond's wife, Ivy, and Cayden's wife, Avery, attending another child's birthday party, the sisters and brothers were on their own.

They had enjoyed one of John's famous food bars, this one of the deluxe taco variety, before gathering in the home's upscale game room. During a major Mona-Mandated renovation, their grade school and high school favorites—such as the well-worn green felt-covered Ping-Pong and pool tables, the seventy-five-inch magnetic dartboard, half-scaled 3D

amusement-themed quality rides and a slew of Wii games—
had disappeared. A cedarwood chess table and pieces had
been replaced by a customized titanium table hosting king,
queen, rook and the rest of the gang cast in sterling silver
and eighteen-carat gold. Desmond and Jake enjoyed a game
of pool using crystal-covered sticks on a CueLight table
with LEDs that created a visual show by following the path
of the balls. There were only five such tables in the world.

A one-hundred-and-eighteen-point surround sound system enveloped the room with concert-quality blends of '70s
and '80s pop, rock and R&B, a nod to their parents' era.

Jake studied his brother even as he studied the table. He
passed his stick over an electro-magnetic balancer that replaced messy blue chalk and eyed a purple solid.

"I don't know him well enough to form that strong of
an opinion."

Desmond rested his chin on his cue stick and watched
Jake sink the ball.

"In the short time I spent with him, other than representing a respected family that has unbelievably come out
against us, he seemed like a likable, talented, authentic guy."

Reign, sitting at a fully restored collector's item blackjack table from Las Vegas's famed Flamingo Hotel (an au-
tographed photo of the Rat Pack playing blackjack at the
table hung on the wall) paused her near-constant cell-phone
interaction. "*Likable* is an understatement. The man is all
kinds of gorgeous, a god. But with inviting him over, I do
have to wonder, sis…what the heck were you thinking?"

"The Duberry heirs have basically called us thieves,"
Desmond concluded. "And this guy has agreed to try to help
them prove their case."

As was often the case, the Eddingtons' conversation
sounded like a singular mind voicing parts of itself through
different voices. Maeve followed the narrative easily and
completely. They felt as she thought they would. Still, she

gave each sibling her undivided attention. There was no room to get better if one felt they knew it all.

She reached for her glass of full-bodied red wine, grateful that a week had passed before this conversation, giving her plenty of time to mount a defense, where really there was none. That she'd looked forward to secretly salivating over his *all kinds of gorgeous* was probably not an acceptable excuse.

"There was a method to my madness," she easily replied, after taking a sip of her drink. "Keeping my friends close and my enemies closer. Watching an opponent in a social environment can sometimes foreshadow how they'll conduct themselves in court."

Jake shot a lopsided grin in Maeve's direction. "If his social skills are any indication, you'd better brush off your law books."

"Thanks for your vote of confidence," Maeve deadpanned.

Reign, whose thumbs had rarely stopped tapping the face of her cell phone, finally set down her phone and wrapped her fingers around a mug of green mint tea flavored with warm spices and vanilla almond milk.

"No matter his actions, he'll be the sexiest guy in the room. I have no doubt about that."

The astute comment rankled Maeve way more than it should have, or that she was prepared to admit. A flurry of email and text exchanges had happened between them, and a meeting for pre-litigation had been set, but Maeve hadn't seen Victor all week. One could have assumed that time apart would have helped to dim the image of how great he looked at last Sunday's brunch. It hadn't. Each night since then as she'd closed her eyes, a vision of his masculine perfection had floated from the recesses of her mind and into her dominant dreamtime thoughts. His mysterious, observant eyes, surrounded by long curly lashes. Strong nose. Full lips. Winking dimple. Hard chest. Silky skin. Big everything. For Maeve, Victor was a sexual encounter waiting to happen just from

the neck up, but if she allowed her eyes to travel and linger…
all bets were off!

She walked over to a fridge and retrieved a bottle of
water. From behind her, Desmond asked, "What's the plan?"

She unscrewed the cap, took a satisfying gulp. "Facts,
plain and simple. I trust our finance department and the
accounting they've presented. During the upcoming meeting, I'm hoping Victor will realize the futility of continuing
forward with what the Duberrys have claimed and agree
to come to an amicable resolution."

That was her hope, and by Wednesday of the following week, the day of the pre-litigation, Maeve had all but
convinced herself that what she desired would be the case.
She walked into the judge's chambers with a junior counsel
representative and three members of the Eddington Enterprise finance team feeling calm and confident. Her wardrobe choice reflected her mood—an eggplant-colored suit
consisting of a bolero-styled jacket and pencil skirt with
a slit up the back, matching pumps, a floral silk blouse
and intricately-carved earrings. Her hair was flat-ironed
to perfection. A teardrop amethyst wrapped in copper was
her only jewel.

They'd arrived to meet Victor and the Duberry heirs,
a meeting she thought would take an hour tops. As with
most mediations, compromise was necessary on both sides
for a timely, least painful resolution. The Eddington team
had put together a deal they felt more than fair, where no
culpability would be admitted by either party in exchange
for a dollar amount that reflected all had been heard. Lillian Duberry had been one of her father's first clients. It
was out of respect for her that the family chose to appease
the younger generation's greed and even possible mismanagement of finances with a one-million dollar increase
(aka, consolation gift) to what was reflected on the Duberry books. Maeve felt a million was a small price to pay

to keep Ms. Duberry's name out of the local papers and to put the whole ordeal behind them.

The team reached the judge's chamber. Maeve braced herself and her hormones for seeing Victor. She entered the room. He wasn't there and dang it if her heart didn't actually sink a little. She covered her disappointment with a genuine smile toward the Duberry heirs, seated on a row of leather chairs. While she didn't know this generation, the Eddingtons and Duberrys had been friends for decades. She'd met them when their dad died and interacted with them again briefly at Lillian Duberry's funeral. They'd been well-mannered and polite. Not one strand of crazy had stuck out on their well-groomed heads. Yet, insanity was present somewhere. It's the only way the claimants could have thought to put *mismanagement* and *Eddington Enterprise* in the same sentence. Even so, the elder Duberry had been revered and supported her father's dream from the beginning. No matter the unfortunate event that brought them together, Maeve would be respectful.

Her colleagues followed her to a row of chairs next to the claimants, separated by a small aisle. Maeve turned to Hubert.

"Hello, I'm Maeve Eddington. These are my colleagues." Introductions were made all around.

"I'm saddened that we're meeting under these circumstances. Your grandmother was a treasured friend to our family, as you know."

Hubert offered a tight smile, curt nod, but said nothing.

Maeve thought his reaction strange but then again, we all grieved differently.

"I knew your father quite well," she continued, making polite conversation. "You favor him."

"Thank you" was his hesitant, softly delivered reply. The young Jada Pinkett–lookalike twin named Adele nudged him in the side.

As awkward as the situation felt, Maeve detected a bit of humanity in his eyes.

"We'll talk to you later," Jada lookalike said without making eye contact.

"I'm only making polite conversation," Maeve responded, proud of herself for the restraint that kept her from adopting the young woman's attitude. "Which twin are you?" she continued, already having known the answer.

"Don't answer," warned the very-reflection-save-for-a-long-bob-styled-hairstyle Jada.

Maeve actually managed to find humor in the situation. *Young'uns.* "Clearly, we have starkly different views about a particular situation. But before I was opposing counsel, I was a good friend to your family. There's no reason to not be civil. We can enjoy a friendly chat, right?"

"Wrong."

The sound of a commanding voice reverberated around the small chambers. Every cell on Maeve's body reacted. Her nipples puckered. Her pussy throbbed. She was as confused as she was excited. Her body had never responded this way at the mere presence of a man. Not with Lionel, the first love two years her senior, who'd been sweet and tender and her everything before cheating on her during a visit to the East Coast. High school sweethearts, their breakup had been agonizing. He'd tried to win her back, and probably would have, except his one-night drunken tryst turned into eighteen years of commitment. The girl had gotten pregnant. Being from a conservative family, the two married and moved to Stanford, California, where he graduated near the top of his class. Grant Nelson hadn't—the pro basketball star she'd dated several years later, who could palm a basketball no problem and had eaten her kitty cat like a dessert. She steeled her body before turning as Victor reached her side.

"I instructed my clients to not speak without my being present. Standard procedure, Counselor, as you well know."

You would think his blatant attempt at a put-down would cool Maeve's desire. Instead, his jab, delivered in a professional voice while caressing her with his eyes, caused muscles in hidden places to contract and release.

"I wasn't speaking to them as an attorney, but as a human being. As *you* well know from our prior conversations, Mrs. Lillian Duberry was a valued family friend. I knew their father my entire life. It was an attempt to get acquainted, nothing more."

Victor's eyes dipped just a bit as he answered, "I look forward to all of us getting to know each other better."

Just then, the back door opened. Judge Doris Keller entered the room. Maeve's heart fell. Keller was the last judge she wanted handling the case.

"Good afternoon, Judge," she said, approaching the diminutive powerhouse. "I thought Judge Ludwig was handling this mediation."

"Got called away," Keller answered. "Family emergency."

Keller looked over Maeve's head at Victor behind them and offered a flirty smile. Maeve all but groaned out loud. Prevailing in this case would be an uphill battle. With her family's reputation on the line, Maeve was there for it.

Wouldn't be easy. He approached the bench, launching her body into action. The space where his hand had touched her while dancing tingled as though it was happening right now. His cologne—light and musky with a hint of spice—tantalized her senses. Raw masculinity and an aura of royalty pulsated around him enveloped Maeve like a love drug on which she could become easily addicted. He'd not touched her, except with his eyes, and yet her body was moist with wanting. Her skin *remembered*. Maeve had heard about those water boys and their magical powers. Had Victor Cortez put a spell on her?

She refocused to hear Judge Keller bringing the mediation to order. Both she and Victor immediately donned their professional masks and presented their sides. The judge listened and took notes but said little. Neither Maeve's finance team nor the heirs were asked to speak. When it became clear that the mediation would not be successful, Keller consulted a tablet on the desk before her and set a date to reconvene in January, after the holidays.

She struck the gavel. *Did she give Victor a wink?* "Court is adjourned."

Maeve returned the files to her tote and reached for her coat. Remembering their earlier conversation, she made no attempt to speak to Victor or the Duberry heirs. Instead, she conversed quietly with her staff as they walked to the parking lot, and then reached her car. She'd exited the space and was about to roll out of the parking lot when her name was called.

"Maeve!"

She looked over to see Victor heading her way, his long, sure strides eating up the concrete. He looked dashing and dangerous, a pair of aviator shades covering those gorgeous lookers, a black leather coat like Morpheus in *The Matrix* flapping behind him in the wind. She tapped the window control.

He rested his arms on the window ledge, his meticulous manliness invading her space. "If I didn't know better—" he began, removing his glasses and fixing her with a penetrating gaze "—I'd think you were running away from me."

I am! she thought. "Don't flatter yourself," she said. "You were occupied with your clients and the meeting was over."

"I would have preferred to reach a settlement." He shrugged his shoulders. "But I'm not surprised you dug in those fly-ass heels you're wearing."

Maeve dared her skin to flush and shifted to lessen the nether reaction his compliment caused.

"Our finance team are very sure of their numbers. We made an offer simply out of respect to Mrs. Duberry."

"My clients are equally convinced that a large amount

of money is missing, has been redirected, reinvested, misplaced or stolen."

"Then I guess we'll see each other in January."

He moved in closer. Maeve wanted to lean away but for the life of her she couldn't move. "I'm hoping to see you much sooner than that."

She closed her eyes. It was broad daylight. They were at the courthouse in the middle of one of the noisiest towns in America. He was her adversary. She didn't care. All she wanted were those thick, luscious lips pressed against hers, for their tongues to dance and the ache within her to subside.

Instead, she heard, "Take it easy, Counselor."

Her wet, slightly parted lips snapped shut and eyes flew open. She may have even been panting. One could never be sure. Now here he was offering a courteous farewell instead of a kiss? Maeve didn't know she could be pissed off and grateful at the same time.

"Will you be returning to Costa Rica?" she heard herself asking, when she could have sworn she meant to say *see you later*.

His eyes darkened in a way that sent a message Maeve was sure she probably shouldn't read. "Most likely." He licked his lips. Maeve found herself following the trail of his tongue like a puppy after his mom. "But I'll be back and forth, to meet with my clients."

"Of course."

"And to see you."

"You're such an inappropriate flirt."

"I'm a red-blooded man attracted to a beautiful woman. I'm not going to deny or hide how I feel about you simply to be politically correct."

"Why am I not surprised."

He smiled and, again, Maeve felt that magnetic pull. He'd straightened and stepped back to see her through the car window. But his presence still seemed to embrace her body as though he hadn't moved.

"You know something? When I think of you, which is often, I remember your beguiling eyes, those sweet, tempting lips, your amazing body. Then I see you and realize my memory has not done you justice. You are an exquisite jewel of a woman, Maeve Eddington. Just want you to know that I recognize it."

With that, he reached through the window, squeezed her arm and walked away without looking back. Maeve managed to put the Aston in gear, a shaky leg pressing the gas to exit the parking lot and put much needed distance between her and who was quickly becoming her personal kryptonite. She could and perhaps should feel many things. Anger. Amusement. Chagrin. Offense. But Victor's words replayed in her head.

He thought of her often. He thought her beautiful, exquisite.

All she felt was giddy, like a love-struck teenager, who simultaneously wished he'd leave her life forever and couldn't wait to see him again.

Eight

Victor swam out of the ocean and traversed the fine grains of white sand in his beachfront backyard. His large manicured feet mounted a thirty-three-step staircase and walked across smooth porcelain stones surrounding his infinity pool. He passed the opened glass wall of his customized paradise to see his housekeeper and pseudo-mother, Hasina, slipping the strap of a large purse over her shoulder.

She stated the obvious. "I was just leaving."

"I see." He continued past her to a glass shelf holding a water pitcher and two crystal goblets. He filled one and drank as Hasina walked toward him.

"Leandro prepared the dinner you requested. You'll remember he had to leave early. His granddaughter has arrived."

Victor lifted his glass in a mock toast. "Ah, so Tarone and Eralia got the girl that they wanted. Congrats to them."

Hasina gave him a look. "They aren't the only ones who should be welcoming children. It is well past time for you to marry and begin a family of your own."

Victor threw an arm around Hasina's shoulder, pulled her close despite her clucks and tsks.

"You know I'm not cut out for marriage," he insisted.

"No man is, until he meets the right woman."

Maeve's smiling face flashed in his mind. He dismissed the thought just as quickly.

Or tried.

But as he sat alone on an upstairs patio overlooking the ocean, dining on an expertly prepared fish dish while watching the sunset, the woman officially known as his opposing counsel stayed on his mind. Once finished with dinner, stoking a cigar and swirling a snifter of premium Scotch, he pulled out his phone and Googled the Eddingtons. News about them was all over the worldwide web. Most notably was an article revealing that the year prior, Maeve's father, Derrick, had been selected as the next president of the Society of Ma'at, an überexclusive business fraternity with influence all over the world. Victor didn't belong to the organization but knew many who did, and understood the kind of power and authority Derrick wielded in that position, the kind of man he had to be to have been chosen for the post. He continued scrolling down the feed and came across an article printed in the society section of the *PDS Post*, Point du Sable's local newspaper. It was an article featuring Derrick and Mona Eddington, their connection to the town and the part they'd played in its auspicious founding. It outlined the humble beginnings of Eddington Enterprise, Derrick and Mona's college courtship, and how the following month, November, they'd celebrate thirty-five years of marriage. A grand celebration at the country club had been planned.

Victor's mind floated back to the Maeve Eddington of his college days, and even better understood how she'd turned out to be the beautiful, intelligent, self-assured woman that she'd become. He imagined a loving two-parent family also successful in business was the perfect type of familial soil for a flower like her to bloom and grow. For him, such stability had not been the case. Arly Cortez, Victor's handsome, extroverted dignitary father, was often absent from the home and played a largely ceremonial parenting role. His mother, Cedella, beautiful but battling insecurities from Arly's roving eye, tried to stay by his dad's side to prevent him from cheating. The result was Victor being largely raised by his *chacha*, the live-in nanny, and a large competent household staff. They were warm, friendly and treated like family. But at the end of the day, they weren't who he needed to receive affection and attention. He needed his mom and dad.

Eventually, his parents divorced. Much later, his mother remarried and now lived a quiet, comfortable life in her family's native Jamaica with an unassuming and devoted mate. His father was on marriage number three with a woman not much older than Victor. Cedella's second time around should have been proof enough for Victor that successful unions were possible. But he tended to focus more on his father Arly's failures, subconsciously nursing a nagging belief that perhaps the apple had not fallen far from the tree.

After a busy time in Costa Rica, which included a side trip to San José, Victor returned to Chicago. Technically, he could have worked from home for another week, but he told himself that it was important to familiarize himself with the world his clients occupied and get a feel for life in Point du Sable. Something about the information on the case he'd gleaned so far still didn't sit right. He wasn't sure what, but a piece to the puzzle seemed to be missing. Time spent in PDS, speaking with the friends and acquaintances of Lillian Duberry and gathering street-level info about her family, specifically the heirs to her fortune, might help him solve the mystery of that missing puzzle piece.

That's what he told himself.

All during the flight on his private jet, while checking into his suite at the Four Seasons and having his rental car delivered to the valet, he allowed himself to believe that, not twenty-four hours back in town, he was heading to the Point du Sable Country Club for business purposes. To rub shoulders with people who may have known Mrs. Duberry, her late son, Hubert Jr., or his three children. Nothing to do with one leggy, alluring, irresistible attorney who thwarted his every advance.

His being back in Illinois early and deciding to work out at the country club instead of the Four Seasons' top-of-the-line fitness center had nothing to do with Maeve Eddington.

Nothing. Nada. Zilch.

Yet, as he was cleared by the doorman and entered the Point du Sable Country Club, Victor was very sure about why he was there. Maeve. She was the only one on his mind.

Following the doorman's instructions, Victor walked down the hall past a gift shop, coffee counter, a cigar room, library and a series of offices to a door leading out to a glass-encased hallway. It was a cold November Monday but the hallway was toasty. He reached the athletic center, quickly changed into workout clothes and rather than go directly to the indoor tennis courts, his ultimate destination, hit the weight room.

Thirty minutes later, as he headed down the hallway toward the courts, fully warmed up and ready to play, a familiar scent teased his nose. He increased his stride, turned the corner, and there she was.

"Maeve."

Turning from the information board she eyed, her surprise was obvious. "Victor?"

"The one and only."

A smirk replaced shock. "What are you doing here?"

"Working out," he replied, a hand sweeping his clothing. His fingers longed to get tangled in her curls, his hand to rub the soft skin peeking out from a tight tee and leggings that emphasized a perfectly round, totally squeezable ass. Instead, he busied them by holding the ends of a towel around his neck.

"What are you doing here?"

"Getting in a good tennis match. Or so I thought."

"You didn't?" She shook her head. "What happened?"

"My partner bailed."

"Who was that?"

"Cornelius."

"Bummer."

Her eyes narrowed. "Have you spoken with him?"

Unlike Maeve's earlier honest reaction, Victor's surprise was feigned. A conversation with Cornelius while en route was how he'd known Maeve was at the club.

"Me? I only arrived in town a short while ago."

She crossed her arms. "And decided to come here to work out."

"Absolutely."

"You couldn't do that at the hotel gym?" A raised brow underscored her skepticism.

"Had I done that, I wouldn't have run into you." Victor could see every one of the wheels turning in that beautiful head of hers. "Besides, when it comes to tennis, I play a decent game."

"Is that so?"

"I'm no Rafael Nadal but I can beat you."

"Ha! Careful, player. Don't let your mouth write a check that your butt can't cash."

"A strong racket is all I need to make a full payment. Unless you're too unsure of yourself to go against someone like me, which I would understand completely."

The air was full of desire. A daring excitement crackled and swirled around them. Victor held his tongue, allowing the silence, knowing Maeve would never walk away from the gauntlet he'd thrown down.

"Full match," she finally said.

"Okay."

"Best two out of three."

"Yes, but each round only to three points."

"Six."

He looked at this watch. "It's a workday."

"Four."

"Okay."

She turned toward a set of double doors nearby. "We'll toss a coin to see who serves first."

"Or you can go first, no problem."

"Oh, no. I will not have it said that you took it easy on me and aided in your own butt-whooping."

It was Victor's turn to laugh. "Your spunkiness is sexy."

"Not spunkiness. Skill."

Once on the court, the two were all business. Victor had no way of knowing that Maeve was an ace tennis player throughout high school. She was equally ignorant of his close friendships with professional tennis stars, or that while growing up he routinely played against them. That he'd been good enough to be scouted and had almost turned pro. Maeve's serves were not as hard as Victor's. But they were well-placed and came with an unpredictable spin. Victor eased up on his service swing a bit, but soon found himself playing all out to keep the game close. When an incredible ace helped her claim the second set, Victor became serious. His competitive nature kicked all the way in. He won the third round handily, four to two. He'd worked up not only a good sweat, but a healthy appreciation for Maeve's court game.

"You're a badass," he said as they left the courts and retrieved bottles of water.

"And you're no novice," Maeve replied, rubbing an arm Victor imagined now sore from bearing the brunt of his hard returns. He felt a bit of remorse.

"I trained for years," he admitted after a long drink of water. "Almost turned pro."

She punched his arm. "No wonder you flung me like a ragdoll, had me running from one side of the court to the other with your line-dusting shots!"

"Most of which you returned, and expertly at that." Victor's look was one of open admiration. "Any woman other than Serena Williams wouldn't have gotten a set off me."

"Not Halep or Coco, or Naomi Osaka?"

Maeve began walking toward the dressing rooms. Victor fell into step beside her.

"Okay, any of those top ten women could probably kick my ass."

Maeve's water bottle paused midway to her mouth. "Careful, Counselor. That almost sounded like humility, something I'm sure a man as arrogant as you can't possibly possess."

"Not true. I'm aware of my strengths as well as my faults."

"Name one. A fault, I mean."

Victor stopped and, after a surreptitious look around, stepped close to her and placed his mouth to her ear.

"I can't seem to get you off my mind."

He pressed a light kiss to her earlobe and heard an intake of breath before being pushed away.

"That's a fault?" she asked, her tone light even though the nipples suddenly outlined on her T-shirt were hard evidence of mutual desire.

"Right now, to be honest, it's one hell of a problem. I very much want to get to know you better, but there's a lawsuit in the way."

They reached an open area with the women's rooms on one end and the men's rooms on the other.

"Which is why as much as I have enjoyed the evening, I think we should limit all future interactions to the courtroom, not the tennis court or this club."

He looked pointedly at the headlights perpetrating as nipples. "Are you sure about that?"

"She looked down, hurriedly crossed her arms over her chest and straightened her spine. "Positive."

"For now, I'll abide by your wishes, Maeve Eddington.

But after winning this case, I'm taking you out, a proper date."

"After losing this case, you might change your mind."

"I won't."

"Lose, or change your mind?"

"Neither." Victor's answer was immediate and without compromise.

A slow smile blessed Maeve's face, and him along with it. "We'll see."

"I guess we will. Next week. Judge's chamber."

Every part of his body wanted every part of hers. He imagined a kiss that began at her toes, traveled slowly upward and lasted all night long. He shut down the thought—quickly, forcibly. They were in public. In the close-knit community of Point du Sable. Where everyone knew each other, the windows had eyes and the walls could talk. They said their goodbyes in the hall. Victor jammed his clothes into a duffel bag and left the club without changing. Once in the car, he sent Maeve a text.

You look as beautiful hot and sweaty as you do cool and collected. Tonight, I'll be dreaming of you.

He pressed Send, quickly, before he had time to weigh the action, or talk himself out of it. Within seconds, his vibrating cell phone signaled the arrival of her response.

Tonight your dream. Tomorrow your nightmare.

Victor laughed heartily, shaking his head as he eased out of the circular drive and drove down the picturesque tree-lined road toward the town's center and the highway on-ramp. He found an easy-listening channel on satellite radio and bobbed a head filled with thoughts of how he could spend time with Maeve outside of the courthouse. He was usually measured, calculating, every move planned. Maeve made him want to forget all that structure, throw caution to the wind.

It was a new concept, both thrilling and terrifying. Victor was up for the ride.

Nine

Maeve sat with Regina Campbell, a dear friend from childhood whom she had seen only sparingly since being a bridesmaid in a spectacular wedding two years ago. They'd run into each other at a recent First Friday Chicago and vowed to get together before the month was out. As they studied menus at the Tasty Vegan, a new upscale restaurant owned by one of Reign's friends, Maeve realized how long it had been since she'd had such a moment, to just relax and chill, and hang out with a friend. In addition to the Duberry case, she was overseeing other matters of the firm's law department, including pending software patents initiated by Cayden Barker, their techie whiz, and the E-Squared cryptocurrency that Desmond had launched the year before. And, of course, there was another stress factor.

Victor Cortez. That manly mass of provocation was never far from her mind.

"Everything on this menu sounds delicious," Regina noted, taking a sip of her Chicago Iced Tea packing a tequila punch. "Do you have any recommendations?"

"I've only been here once before and had the fish tacos. I don't know what plant they're made from, but the combination of the flavorful meat substitute, crunchy slaw and tangy sauce tastes better than real fish! Had me giving serious consideration to turning in my meat-eater card."

"Impressive, considering how much you like meat." Regina wriggled her eyebrows.

"Girl, shut up."

They laughed and scanned the menu. Regina decided to try the tacos. Maeve opted for a new dish, a barbecued cauliflower steak topped with roasted vegetables and chilled mango. It came with a spicy black bean and quinoa combo. With her workout schedule interrupted and the holidays approaching, Maeve figured eating healthy was not only a good idea but necessary if she was going to shimmy into those form-fitting Thanksgiving and Christmas gathering gowns.

"I read the article on your parents," Regina said, once the waiter had placed down a basket of seasoned bread sticks and freshened their waters. "Thirty-five years. Wow!"

"I know, can you believe it?"

"These days, if a marriage lasts thirty-five months, it's considered success."

"Exactly."

"That makes Desmond how old, thirty-one or -two?"

"Thirty-two his next birthday."

"Ooh, which makes somebody I know inching close to the big 3-0."

Maeve reached for her wineglass of sparkling water. "Don't remind me. I only get to be twenty-something for one more year."

"And still single." Maeve nodded. "Any prospects?"

"Not really."

Before that last word was out, Victor's seductive eyes swam into view, accompanied by the sensual words of their last text exchange.

"Ever hear from what's-his-name?"

Regina didn't have to describe whom she meant. *Lionel the Jackal*. In their almost seven years together before breaking up, two of them as a couple she thought happily engaged, Maeve had fondly referred to him as *My Lover Lionel*.

"Nope."

In that one word was a whole conversation. Regina interpreted everything, as only a bestie could, and moved on. "Who's going to be your escort for the anniversary celebration?"

"Good question."

There were any number of men Maeve could ask to accompany her. Colleagues, old classmates, a handful of either of her brothers' friends. Before Peyton arrived, Maeve might have even considered safe and predictable Cornelius. But rumor had it their dating had turned serious in just a few months, with her old friend hinting to soon make their status official. Maeve didn't blame him. In fact, she approved of the idea. The love she had for Cornelius was the kind one had for a brother. It had never been and could never be anything more. *If he could snag a woman as beautiful as Peyton*, Maeve thought, *good for him*.

"What about Cornelius?" Regina asked as though reading Maeve's mind. "You two went out back in the day."

"*Back in the day* being the operative part of that statement. Our time together never went much beyond friendship. Kissing him was like kissing a relative."

"Ew."

"Exactly." Maeve dipped a chunk of freshly baked bread in the restaurant's secret combination of balsamic vinegar, olive oil and African spices. "What about you? Are you and Bryant ready to start a family yet?"

"Yes, and we're working on it as often as we can."

"You always were my freaky friend."

"Takes one to know one."

"No, it doesn't. When it comes to romantic partners, I've always been conservative."

"You're right. Partying, casual hookups, you were never that girl. But, hey, don't knock regular chandelier-swinging, mind-blowing sex until you've tried it."

"No judgment here. I'm happy for you."

"And not with just any man, but the one who feels made

for you. Being married can be difficult but it's worth the challenge. It's a journey of lessons and conscious commitment. I want you to experience it, Maeve, the kind of love your parents have, the kind Bryant and I are striving for."

"Right now my focus is the courtroom, not the bedroom. We're in the middle of a few legal proceedings that are critically important to the company's future."

"Which one of those critical proceedings is going to dance with you this holiday season or keep you warm at night?"

Maeve didn't have a comeback for that. A major eye roll was the next best thing.

"When looking at the future, don't just focus on the company. Focus on you. That's all I'm saying."

"Well said, best friend. Now, can you get out of my business?"

"Yes, for the time being. Just one last thing."

Maeve managed not to huff. Barely. "What."

"Don't stay so focused on making a living that you forget to make a life."

Their food arrived and the conversation moved on, but over the next week, Regina's words stuck with Maeve. Especially whenever she saw Victor, which for whatever reason seemed to be all the time. Twice in the judge's chamber when their case first missed the docket, then changed again because of the court's busy schedule. Once at the club when Victor was there having dinner with Cornelius and a group of people she didn't know. Those times were thankfully public and brief. They also reiterated how physically attracted she was to the man. Too attracted for him to be her escort to the anniversary party. No way could she ask him. It would be neither appropriate nor wise.

But she wanted him there. She could admit that she missed him. The air seemed less vibrant without him around.

By the time Saturday night and the gala arrived, all those thoughts had been pushed aside. Maeve had asked a for-

mer classmate and longtime friend Matthias Bailey to escort her to the dance. Still, she dressed with Victor Cortez
in mind. *Damn him!* The silky copper-colored mermaid-
styled gown that had been custom designed for the occasion, with its peekaboo bodice and side split that would
have given Angelina Jolie a run for her long-legged money,
felt soft and sensuous against her skin, the way Victor's
hands did when he held her. The stilettos that graced her
feet added confidence along with height. Completing her
glammed-out look took a village that had playfully coined
themselves the "Maeve Makeover Team," but when she slid
onto the buttery seats of the limousine that Matthias had
arranged for their transport, Maeve felt like Cinderella on
her way to the ball.

They arrived at the country club and entered a lobby
awash in ball gowns, tuxedos and jewels that no doubt ri-
valed the queen's collection. Yes, the one in England. Any
newbie would have been awed, even intimidated by the
scene. But for Maeve, these were her people, friends and
peers, in the place that had been a home away from home
since being the belle of her own tenth birthday ball. Having also grown up in Point du Sable, Matthias was equally
comfortable. Soon, when he was pulled into a lively political
conversation with a budding congressman, Maeve continued around the club's expansive lobby, where guests were
enjoying predinner cocktails and appetizers offered by uni-
formed staff. She laughed easily, hugged sincerely and accepted congrats on behalf of her parent's thirty-five years
of wedded bliss. Then, something happened. The room's
temperature changed. Somehow she felt—knew—that Victor was near her. She tried to convince herself such feelings
were foolish. But they lingered, increased. She turned toward the restroom and a quick moment to pull herself together and there he was. Her foolish fantasy in the flesh.

"Hello, beautiful."

"V-Victor."

Who in the hell was this stuttering woman? Maeve had never done so a day in her life! Victor's smile suggested he figured that as well, and that he was the reason for her discomfort. Rather than back off or leave her presence altogether so that she could breathe again, he added insult to injury by leaning toward her, planting a faint kiss on her cheek and speaking softly against her ear.

"You look absolutely decadent."

Maeve prided herself on not taking a step back. She was not some withering wallflower and he was no god, even though she was quite certain he could play one on TV. He was a tall, strong, handsome man, like dozens of others she'd met. Okay, maybe ten. She couldn't lie to herself. She'd never been in the presence of a man that made her feel the way Victor did. Like at this very moment she could lose all sense of decorum, pull him into a broom closet and shag him like a rabbit in heat.

"What are you doing here?"

His raise of a thick perfectly arched eyebrow added to his debonair looks and rakish charm. To look that good in a simple tuxedo should be illegal in all fifty states.

"I was invited by—"

"There you are!"

A very attractive woman, wearing a beautiful red dress that showcased her bountiful cleavage and hugged her curves before flaring into a skirt made of what looked to be all the tulle in Chicago, snaked her arm possessively through Victor's and glued herself to his side. Maeve was initially thankful for the interruption...until her eyes settled on the woman's face, the one with eyes now looking up dreamily at Victor as though he were that god Maeve had thought didn't exist only seconds before.

"Come with me, handsome," she said as though Maeve weren't standing there. "I have some very important people I'd like you to meet."

Victor subtly shifted his body away from the woman and reclaimed his arm. "Camela, do you know Maeve?"

Camela gave Maeve a dismissive sweep with her eyes before tossing what looked to be at least eight packs of premium Indian weave across a smooth bare shoulder touting a flower tattoo.

"Of course I know her. Hello, Maeve," she managed, between lips tight enough to dam Niagara Falls.

"Good evening, Camela." Maeve bit back a chuckle and offered a smile, while also making a mental note to curse out her brother Jake, Camela's classmate and the assumed reason she'd been invited, at the first opportunity.

"Victor, let's go."

The shift in Victor's mood was subtle and striking at the same time. His facial expression barely changed yet he seemed not to breathe. Clearly, this wasn't a man used to being told what to do, nor one who took orders kindly. He took a step away from Camela and faced her directly.

"I need to speak with Maeve privately. Head on over to where your friends are. I'll join you shortly."

"But I want—"

"Or I can bypass dinner altogether and call it an early night."

"No need to do that, handsome. I'll, um, I'll be right over there." Camela pointed across the room to a group standing near the closed dining room doors. She squeezed his arm and blew a kiss before sauntering away. If her swaying hip show was for Victor, Camela would have been disappointed because when Maeve looked over at him, his eyes were on her.

"You might want to check your digits," she said.

"Excuse me?"

"You know…fingers, toes, moving body parts. Camela is quite the man-eater. I've known her to chew men up and spit them out before they even knew they were on the menu."

He took a step toward her and reached for her hand.

"I assure you that all of my body parts are accounted for and in prime working order. I've met the Camela types a time or two and trust me, I can handle her."

"I don't doubt that. How'd you end up as her date? Not that it's my business but…"

"I have no secrets. When it comes to my personal life, you can ask whatever you want."

"Really?"

"Anything."

"I'll keep that in mind."

"As for Camela, I met her here earlier this week while having lunch with Cornelius and a few of his colleagues. He warned me not to accept her invite to your parents' anniversary."

"Then why did you?"

"It was clear that you were too scared to follow your heart and invite me yourself, so in order to spend time socially in your beautiful presence, a brother had to do what a brother had to do."

Maeve's quick comeback took a slow bus. Victor's bull's-eye statement rendered her speechless.

"Tell me I'm lying."

"I'll tell you that you're arrogant." *And accurate.*

"I'll tell you that I'd love to caress your body the way that dress is doing."

"And I'll tell you that you are being wholly inappropriate, and it's not appreciated."

Victor gave a mock sigh. "There you go, lying to yourself again. Besides, I'm not approaching you in a professional capacity right now."

True, but Maeve didn't feel the need to tell him that.

"Tell me that you're not attracted to me, that you don't want me as much as I want you."

"What either of us wants doesn't matter. We're opposing counsel on a serious matter concerning my family, which makes you off-limits."

"Says who?"

"Me."

"I know why. It's because a woman like you is used to being in control and a man like me might prove too much to handle."

"Your ego is unduly inflated."

"Prove it."

"I don't have to prove anything."

"One kiss."

"Excuse me?"

"Let's share one kiss. If after that you still feel my advances inappropriate and unwanted, I'll back off and be the height of decorum from here on out."

"And if I don't, you'll continue to be a pain in the ass?"

Victor generated one of his devastating, award-worthy smiles.

"Never mind. I knew you weren't as brave as you pretended to be. Plus—" Victor nodded in a direction behind her "—looks like our prolonged conversation is making your date antsy."

Without turning around, Maeve responded, "I could say the same about yours. Camela has been staring over here with such a fiery gaze I'm surprised there's not a hole burned into your back. Or at least a patch of that tuxedo on fire."

Victor reached for her hand and gave it a squeeze. Such an innocent act should not have threatened to set her bush aflame but she swore a bonfire could have been stoked from her snatch.

"Enjoy your evening, Ms. Eddington."

Maeve slid her hand out of Victor's grasp and turned without another word. She prided herself on walking, not running, as far away from him as quickly as possible. Didn't matter. He stayed on her mind. Through the appetizer and the entrée. Through the speeches, laughter and tears. During the toasts and razzing of her parents. Finally, with dessert on the way, Maeve sent texts to Victor, Cayden's wife, Avery, and the last one to Reign.

I'm sneaking out to speak with Victor. If I'm not back in fifteen minutes, give a rescue call.

Within a nanosecond of hitting the send button, Maeve was sure she'd lost her mind. But after one kiss with the man who dared underestimate her, she was sure she'd find it again.

Ten

As Victor sat through Camela's prattle, he decided Maeve owed him big-time. A kiss at the very least. He now fully understood why Cornelius warned him against his date's invitation. Camela had barely stopped talking the entire night, even while eating. He wondered how she'd not keeled over dead as, for her, taking breaths between bites or sentences seemed optional. The only saving grace had been the rare moments of reprieve he received from one of Jake's college buddies who also knew Cornelius and was seated next to him. Unlike Victor, however, this guy was totally into his date, so conversation between the two guys was limited. The evening wore on, further dampened by his inability to spend any real time with Maeve who sat resplendent at the head table next to a guy who was probably completely likable but whom Victor wished right now to either trade places with or punch in the throat. Just as he concluded slitting one's wrist was probably less painful than another five minutes seated next to Camela, his cell phone vibrated. He retrieved it from his suit's inside pocket and checked it discreetly.

Meet me in five. Through the lobby. Down hall beside coat check. Out emergency exit. Across grass to adjacent building. Make sure no one sees you. I'll only wait five minutes.

Victor's heart leaped. His groin tightened. He immediately stood, excused himself from the table and strode away without a backward glance. Dinner had just completed so very few people mingled in the lobby. That a set of bathrooms was in the hallway Maeve had mentioned gave him further cover. He ducked in long enough to wash his hands, then said a quick prayer that when he opened the door the coast would be clear. It was. He reached the emergency exit and, after sending up another plea to the man in the moon, quickly pressed down the latch and held his breath. No alarm. So far so good.

Stepping outside took his breath away. It was at least below freezing and felt likely below zero. Not cold enough to dash the heat he felt for Maeve. Seeing a light on in a nearby building, he took another quick look around and dashed toward a set of doors, staying as close to the wall and away from security lights as possible. He reached the unlocked door within seconds, stepped inside and ducked into a darkened hallway.

Before he could formulate a whisper, he smelled her. Smiling, he waited. Blew into his hands to knock off the chill before sliding them into his pockets for more warmth. And then she was there, cloaked in darkness, her body mere inches from his.

"I'm here," he said, instantly feeling foolish for stating the obvious.

"I see."

Her breathy answer came out in a rush. Was it a case of nerves or was she as excited as he was?

"What do you want?"

"To prove I'm not a coward."

"How?"

One step and Maeve closed the distance between them. "Like this."

Feeling Maeve's body press against his sent him on a near-out-of-body experience, as though he were both experiencing the moment and seeing it, too. His arms automatically came up to encompass her waist. His head lowered to her warm, waiting, accessible mouth. Their lips barely touched before hers parted, a clear invitation to deepen the exchange. He wasted no time in doing just that. With a groan, his hand slid up her back and buried itself in the thick tresses at the nape of her neck, gently pulling her head even closer as he slid his tongue inside and tasted heaven. Forcing himself to go slow, he took a moment to plant kisses on her lips, cheek and neck before returning to their tongue tango and setting up a slow sensual pace that matched the speed of his hand sliding down her back to cup the round ass he so admired, squeezing the cheeks gently as he plundered her mouth. To his delight, Maeve wasn't shy. She placed her arms around his neck and crushed her breasts against his chest. It was the perfect position for the journey from her ass to continue to the silky fabric beneath the feathery bodice, fabric that did nothing to hide her pebbled nipples ripe for flicking and pinching ever so slightly and more. He wanted more. Of her. Of this. Of everything. He searched for and found the opening that allowed his hand to cup her weighty breast, to run a thumb over the nipple he wanted to suck. Maeve made a sound in her throat that fanned the flame burning in his crotch, making his dick as hard as stone. In this moment, he could think of nothing more fitting than getting naked—here, now—and making love to her all night long. He didn't care that they were missing a party. Screw Camela and her incessant talk. Everything he wanted was right here in his arms.

With the full intention of giving them what he knew they both wanted, he lifted Maeve off the ground, turned them around and placed her against the wall. Her legs automatically wound themselves around his hips. The long slit in her dress gave him perfect access to her paradise. He didn't ask for nor wait for an invitation to slip inside. With one hand firmly around her waist, his other hand slid between the velvety fabric of her silver dress. To his delight, Maeve wore stockings held up by a garter belt. Magnificent and so incredibly sexy. Who wore garters these days? All Victor knew was that he was grateful that the minuscule device was perfect for what he wanted to do, which was slide his fingers along the satiny soft skin of Maeve's inner thigh. She gasped. He thrust his tongue deeper into her mouth while moving his hand ever closer to the feminine flower covered only by a scanty piece of lace. Pushing aside the thong he ran his middle finger along the slit between her already wet folds, then slid the digit between them. Maeve clutched him tighter, swirling her tongue as he swirled his finger before thrusting it deep inside her.

"Ahhh!" Maeve's head shot back and connected with the wall.

Thump.

Everything stilled. Maeve broke the kiss. "Stop," she managed, her head resting on his shoulder. "Put me down."

Victor reluctantly removed his finger from between her dewy folds and slid her body down the length of his and over the solid evidence of his desire.

"Baby," he whispered, planting kisses on every available inch of skin. "I want you. We both want this. Let's—"

Maeve placed a hand on his chest. "No. We need to get back to the party. That's—" She swallowed, stepped around him and began rearranging her clothes. "That's what we need to do. It's the only thing we should do right now."

Victor watched a myriad of emotions play across her face, saw the exact moment control was regained and her professional social butterfly mask slipped in place. "Maeve…"

"Did anyone see you come here?"

He sighed. "No."

"Are you sure?"

"As sure as anyone can be about these things."

She began walking down the hall opposite from how

he'd arrived. "Come on. There's another door with a walk that leads around to the lobby entrance. You go that way. I'll go back the way we both came. If anyone is watching, we'll arrive back from different directions."

They reached the door. He turned to her, placed a hand on her arm. "You know this isn't over."

"There is no *this*," she responded, pulling away from his grasp. "You asked for a kiss and got way more than that."

"I didn't force you to do anything you didn't want to do."

"No, you didn't. We're both adults. I have no regrets. But from here on out, our interactions must remain totally professional."

Victor laughed out loud. "After what we just experienced? Are you serious?"

"As serious as mandated mask wearing. Can I trust you to behave yourself?"

The situation was no longer a laughing matter, Victor decided. He stepped close enough in the darkened hallway to see every detail of her face. "Absolutely not, sweetheart. This party is just getting started."

With that parting shot, he pushed the door open and stepped outside, welcoming the blast of cold that shot through his body. Quickly ascertaining where he was, he began walking toward the lobby entrance. He barely felt the ground beneath him. Being with Maeve, remembering the feel of her body melded to his, the taste of her lips, the warmth of her sex made him feel as though he were in heaven, walking on clouds. He raised his hand to his nostrils and inhaled her scent. His thoughts were everywhere and singular, all at once. Everywhere concerning what had just happened and how he could make sure it became a regular part of his life. Singular on Maeve Eddington, and a determination to make her his.

One step inside the lobby took him from heaven to hell. Camela, who'd been speaking with one of the guards, made a beeline in his direction, then fell in step beside him. Her move caused Victor to change his mind about returning to the party. He headed for the coat check instead.

Camela stayed by his side. "Victor! I was worried. Where have you been?"

"Taking care of an urgent matter."

He glanced over and noted Camela's narrowed eyes. "With Maeve?"

"With the business associate who texted me."

It wasn't a lie. He and Maeve were handling business, albeit on opposite ends of a lawsuit. In the future, they'd be handling much more pleasure than business together, if Victor had his way.

They reached the coat check.

"What are you doing?" Camela demanded.

"Retrieving my coat."

"Why? The party is just getting started."

Victor smiled at the irony of her words, the ones he'd uttered to Maeve just moments ago.

"Sorry, darling. Emergency. Can't be helped."

Emergency, indeed. He needed to get home and take a cold shower.

"I was looking forward to checking out your moves on the dance floor. But I don't mind us continuing the party in private to see what other moves you have." She opened her clutch, retrieved her coat ticket and presented it to the clerk.

Victor stayed her hand. "I'm leaving. You should stay and enjoy the rest of the celebration, get your dance groove on, like you said." He gave his ticket to the clerk.

"You want to leave without me?"

"I'd hate for your good time to end due to my unexpected interruption."

"You brought me here. I was your date!"

"Correction. I was your date."

"You can't expect me to stay here alone!"

He shrugged. "It's up to you. And I do apologize but I can't stay, nor can I give you a ride home. I'll arrange for a limousine service to be on call to pick you up at whatever time you choose and take you wherever you need to go."

"Maeve!"

Both Victor and Camela turned as Maeve entered the lobby from the far hallway and smiled at the young man who'd called her name. If she saw Victor at the coat check, she showed no sign, but laughed and threw her arm around the guy's shoulder as they headed toward the ballroom. Victor tried not to stare but his eyes had other plans. Thankfully, the clerk brought his coat, bringing him out of the trance.

He pulled out a card and held it out to Camela. "This is my driver. I'll inform him of your impending call and instruct him to chauffer you anywhere for the next twenty-four hours."

Camela snatched the card.

"I know this evening hasn't gone as you may have hoped. I do thank you for inviting me. For whatever it's worth, I enjoyed myself."

He turned and walked toward the valet, hoping to be rid of her.

No such luck.

"You think you can dump me just like that?" she snarled.

"I'm not dumping you, Camela. I'm ending our date early."

She spun around quickly and but for the five-inch stilettos Victor was sure she would have stomped away. He felt badly for her disappointment, but not enough to put himself through any more torture in the presence of her company. That would only tarnish the time he'd spent with Maeve, a memory he'd tuck away for safe keeping until he could convince her to make more moments like that. Victor was certain that that would happen. Their relationship had as much chance of staying "strictly professional" as he had of winning the lottery without buying a ticket. No chance at all. Victor watched his car pull into the circular drive and strolled to the door with confidence. He wasn't much of a betting man. Even so, he loved those odds.

Eleven

For the rest of the night Maeve had only one thought. Victor. She tried to forget their encounter but couldn't, as her mind replayed a video of their stolen moments over and over again. His tongue hot, forceful and delicious inside her mouth. She'd wanted him to be an inept kisser, a clumsy lover. He was exactly the opposite. She'd planned for the exchange to be brief, really, just a peck. But for the life of her, when their lips touched, all she could do was open her mouth and twirl her tongue around his, place her arms around his neck and give in to the moment. When he pulled her more firmly against his chest, her body had rejoiced, had sang hallelujah as one strong arm secured her against him while the other had glided down her back, over her ass and stayed there. She'd felt his burgeoning desire press against her, had imagined the feel of him deep inside her. The thought had caused a sensation to swirl between her thighs, for her yoni to dampen and her nipples to pebble. And when he'd made the manly move of picking her up as though she were a feather, holding her against the wall and sliding a finger inside her? It's a wonder she didn't have an orgasm right then. Just thinking about it had her almost having one now.

"Maeve?"

Matthias's voice seemed to come from a distance. She turned to him. "Huh?"

He frowned. "Did you hear me?"

"No, what did you say?"

"I asked if you were okay."

No! Hell, no! I'm sooo not okay. Unless she could get Victor out of her system—and yes, he was definitely in there—Maeve doubted she'd ever be okay again.

"Of course, I'm okay. Why would you ask?"

"Because I called your name," he replied rather pointedly. "Twice. And you didn't answer."

"I'm sorry, Matt. My mind must have wandered."

"Seems like it's been wandering all night. I might as well be on a date with a ghost."

Maeve forced herself fully into the present. When she turned to him, her heart was sincere.

"I'm really sorry. You're right. My body's here but my mind has been on…other things."

"Want to talk about it?"

She shook her head. "Work stuff, which at this party to celebrate my parents is the last thing I should be thinking about."

Standing, she reached for his hand. "Want to dance?"

"I don't know…"

"Come on. Please!"

Normally, she wouldn't beg anyone to boogie, but his hesitant pouting was well-deserved.

"Oh, okay."

She led the way to the middle of the dance floor and forced herself to get lost in the loud dance music flowing from the speakers. She managed to almost forget about Victor's skilled fingers and lethal kisses, and was actually able to give her date the attention he deserved. She laughed with her mom, joked with Reign and her brothers, danced with her dad and joined what appeared to be everyone at the celebration as they swarmed the floor to do the Electric Slide. At the end of the night, she and Matthias made comfortable small talk as they waited for the town car to make its way to the lobby doors in a circular drive now crowded with limos, Bentleys, Maybachs and other luxury rides. Finally, their car reached the doors. They dashed into the cold and scurried inside its warm confines.

"That was awesome!" Matthias said, settling against the car's supple leather back seat.

"I agree. Tons of fun. My parents deserved every minute."

"Looks like you did, too." He reached over and grabbed her hand. "You always were a workaholic."

Maeve removed her hand from his and made a show of adjusting her coat as though that were the reason. From the look on Matthias's face, he wasn't fooled.

"Tonight was proof that I need to change that. There are a couple heavy cases on my plate but I'm definitely going to add a lighter workload to my New Year resolutions."

The town car made its way through the maze of vehicles and finally reached the road. Matthias checked his watch. "It's a bit late but can I interest you in a nightcap? My flight leaves early tomorrow."

His expression was hopeful. Maeve felt like a jerk, but she couldn't lead him on. Not with the imprint of Victor's fingers still fresh on her sex.

"I'm sorry, Matt, but Mom and Dad are leaving tomorrow, too. They're going away on a fourteen-day cruise. I'm sure she'll need my help with last-minute packing."

Matthias's back straightened. His smile disappeared.

"Matt, you and I have always been great friends. I hope that never changes."

"What if I'd like to be more than friends?"

"That's not possible," she said with a shake of her head. "Especially now. Work is taking up all of my time, plus some I don't have. There's no room for a relationship."

"I hope this isn't about Lionel. What he did to you was awful. But I always thought you were much too good for him. Forgive me for being blunt, but I think it's past time for you to move on with your life. I'd love to be the man on that journey."

Her cell phone rang. She reached into her clutch and checked the screen. *Victor!* Darn it. Talk about bad timing. She silenced the ringer and dropped the phone back into her purse.

"Work-related?" Matthias asked with a skeptically arched brow.

"Family. I'll see them soon."

Hearing the words she'd spoken out loud did funny things to her gut. A part of her considered a world where Victor was family. All of her wanted to see him again, the sooner the better. *Only in court*, she told herself. Seeing him again in private would be the worst thing she could ever do.

That's what she planned to reiterate when the car dropped her off, and once undressed and settled into bed, she rang Victor's number. That he answered on the first ring had her all out of sorts.

"Still thinking of me?" was his cocky greeting.

"Just returning your call." Adding a yawn couldn't have made Maeve's greeting sound more nonchalant, but she did so anyway.

Good girl.

"What did you want?" She knew it was the wrong question to ask before the words had left her mouth.

"You."

"Not happening."

"You can honestly say that you don't want me, after what we experienced tonight."

"With every fiber of my being." Her honesty was as liberating as it was surprising. "But we don't always get what we want."

"We're two consenting adults who want to enjoy pleasure together. What's wrong with that?"

"I can think of a million reasons."

"Name one."

"Lillian Duberry."

"You can't separate work from your personal life?"

"By turning down your continued invitation for amazing sex, that's exactly what I'm doing."

"So you admit the sex would be amazing, huh?"

His voice was low, almost hot, in her ear. Her pelvic muscles contracted. She shifted, squeezed her legs together and demanded her body behave.

"Obviously, you've got skills. Now wipe that smug smile off your face."

He laughed, which sent shots of warmth tumbling into her belly.

"Damn right, I'm smiling. I want to rock your world, girl."

Maeve slid down and adjusted the pillows. She loved talking to a manly man like Victor. She was also überaware that if he were as persistent a lawyer as he was a potential lover, she was in deep trouble, and would have to bring her A-plus game to win the company's case.

"Come see me."

Desire dripped off the three simple words, now infused with a trace of the Caribbean lilt she found hard to resist.

She resisted.

"No, I can't. I won't."

"Why not?"

"On top of the reasons I've already told you, repeatedly, a visit isn't wise."

"Even at this late hour?"

"Especially now. Chicago may look big but it's a small town. Everyone knows me and each building has eyes."

"Then come home with me. To Costa Rica. Away from professional obligations and prying eyes. Maeve, baby, let's stop fighting the inevitable. Life is short. Tomorrow isn't promised. Let's give ourselves a chance to experience something amazing."

"Now is not the time for a vacation."

A lame-sounding response even to her own ears. *Really, chick. That's all you've got?*

"You can't be planning to work through the holidays. Even flourishing companies like Eddington Enterprise have to close their doors sometime. Thanksgiving is a time for family but what about Christmas? Or leaving the day after and celebrating the New Year there? We could bring it in with our own fireworks. Pack a bag. That's all. I'll handle everything else. Or bring nothing but your beautiful self and I'll add a shopping spree to our plans."

Maeve flopped on her back. "I'll think about it," she finally said.

"I fly out next week, so you'll have the space to do so."

"Okay. We'll talk later."

"Good night, beautiful."

Maeve turned out the light. Sleep was elusive. *Join him in Costa Rica? That man has gone crazy!*

She thought this, but somewhere deep in the recesses of her traitorous mind Maeve was already packing her bags.

"You're thinking about going where, to do what?"

It was the morning after her parents' anniversary celebration. The standard brunch with friends had been canceled. The siblings were on their own. Desmond and his wife, Ivy, had used the opportunity for a quick "day away" to Memphis for blues and barbecue. Jake was spending the day with his girlfriend of the week. Maeve decided to chill and do nothing. She was happy when little sis, Reign, decided to join her. So much so that she'd just blabbed about an idea she'd not planned to share with anyone.

"I probably won't," Maeve continued, around a bite of perfectly cooked root vegetables highlighting the season that the chef had thoughtfully included in a brunch basket delivered a short while ago. "But it has been a while since I've taken a vacation and so far I have no plans for bringing in the New Year so..."

She shrugged and took another bite of food, chasing it down with cranberry-flavored sparkling water.

Reign's eyes gleamed as she eyed Maeve over a glass of champagne. "I knew you wouldn't be able to pass up all that sweet chocolate. You should go and you should celebrate. Every day and in every position—"

"Sister!"

"I mean every *way* imaginable. Seriously, Maeve. Not only is Victor an eligible bachelor but in either Celsius or Fahrenheit, he's off-the-scale hot! I'd do him in a New York minute."

Maeve scowled.

Reign hurriedly continued. "If he were interested, that is, which he clearly isn't. At least not in me."

"But what about professional protocol? To say dating opposing counsel is unethical is putting it lightly."

"What's unethical about spending time with a guy you find interesting? Are you going to use your wiles to black-mail him into dropping the lawsuit? Do something profes-sionally unseemly behind his back? No. You're going to go to Costa Rica to get the cobwebs blown out of your hoo-ha and I for one say it's about damn time."

Little sister was right, Maeve reluctantly admitted. The following week, she sent Victor a text.

Regarding Costa Rica, offer accepted.

On the morning of December 26, Maeve woke with mixed emotions. A part of her felt alive in a way she'd never expe-rienced. The other part felt uncomfortable with not being in total control. Victor had invited her to Costa Rica, but when questioned about what to pack or their planned activities, his descriptions had been vague.

"You won't need much in the way of clothing," he'd boldly predicted.

Maeve had argued to the contrary, even as her traitor-ous kitty purred.

She packed for a seven-day stay and included an assort-

ment of workout clothes, a variety of bathing suits, a few
sundresses and a silky semi-formal, wide-legged jumpsuit
with crystal beading that felt as good as it made her look
while in it. She thought of wearing it, five-inch pumps and
nothing beneath it, and then after a night of dancing, shed-
ding it to step into Victor's waiting, well-defined arms.
Her body hummed and moistened as visual images filled
her mind.

She had breakfast with the family, who thankfully hadn't
drilled her about the "old friend" she was flying out to visit.
Only Reign knew the identity of said college chum. Desmond drove her to the airstrip for the private plane Victor
had chartered. By the time the Bombardier Global 7500
sailed beyond the snow-filled cloudiness that covered Point
du Sable into the sun-filled sky beyond them, Maeve was
more thrilled than terrified, more curious than cautious
about the decision she'd made. Two flutes of Dom Pérignon
mimosas later, she decided to for once try to turn off her
logical mind and go with the Costa Rican flow.

When they landed, Victor was the first sight she saw.
One for sore eyes. One that could make a blind woman see.
He was the kind of fine one thought couldn't get better but
when he greeted Maeve in all-white casual linen, Maeve
swore his handsome meter had gone higher than the tux in
Chicago, and the meter that night had gone off the charts.
He literally looked good enough to eat, like the chocolate
fudge bars she used to get from the local ice-cream truck
wrapped in shiny white paper—gooey, dripping goodness,
waiting for her willing and salivating tongue.

Just like back in the good old days, said tongue was
now willing, salivating and wanting to lick a big chunk of
chocolate. Thank goodness for the shades that hid the lust
she was positive showed in her eyes.

"Happy holidays!" he greeted, planting a luscious kiss
smack dab on her lips as he picked her up and whirled her
around.

He slid her—slowly, firmly—down the length of his hard, chiseled frame.

Maeve stepped away, looking around suspiciously as soon as her toes touched the ground. "Stop! Someone might see us."

"Relax, sweetheart," Victor replied, keeping his arm securely around her shoulder as he directed a nearby worker to gather her luggage. He reached for her hand and led them toward a gleaming white Jeep.

"This is a private airstrip on private land. Mine. Every eye watching is on my payroll and maintains the strictest of confidences. Although I'm sure they're gawking and I must admit… I'd have it no other way. You're much too gorgeous to hide."

The comment left the very womanly Maeve feeling all girlie inside.

"Thank you for inviting me to your country. What I've seen so far is amazing."

He stopped, suddenly. "Don't tell me this is your first trip to Costa Rica."

"Guilty as charged," Maeve managed with a coy smile. "My parents and brothers have been here, though, and were duly impressed. I've planned to visit for a long time."

"What stopped you?"

"Work, mainly."

They reached the Jeep. The worker placed Maeve's luggage in the back while Victor opened the passenger door before getting in on the driver's side. Once buckled in and on the road, the conversation continued.

"When is the last time you had a vacation?"

"This past summer, I spent a weekend in Sag Harbor. And sometimes I add a day of leisure to business trips."

"I'm talking about a real vacation, like this stay is going to be."

Maeve furrowed her brow. "A couple years ago, maybe? Honestly, I can't remember."

"You've heard the cliché all work and no play."

"I try and maintain balance in my life. Admittedly, the past six months have been busy but by the time summer gets here, things should slow down. The spoils of war from winning the Duberry case will afford me a luxurious and much-needed vacation."

Victor expertly guided the Jeep with one hand while giving Maeve a once-over. "War? Is that what you call it? Is that how you define our relationship?"

"We have no relationship." Maeve paused, pulled a scrunchie from her purse and tamed her wind-whipped curls. "You're opposing counsel, nothing more."

Victor's laugh wrapped around her like an old well-worn sweater.

"You may not know it yet, pretty lady, but I'm much more than that."

Maeve tilted her head as she looked at him. "Are you always so cocky?"

"Only when warranted."

"And you believe that now is one of those times?"

Victor slid his hand down her arm and rubbed his thumb along her wrist. Maeve tried to remain calm but couldn't hide the rapid heartbeat he'd surely felt.

His knowing smile confirmed her thought. "I'll do my best to make it so and let you be the judge."

Yeah, right. That oh-so-sexy Victor Cortez would do his best was exactly what Maeve was afraid of.

Twelve

Victor turned down a palm tree-lined path with an automated security gate that opened upon his arrival.

"*Bienviendos* to Cortez Castle," he announced with a sweep of his arm. "*Mi casa es su casa*."

"Where is it?"

After ascending up a mountain and rounding a final curve, Victor's twenty-three-thousand square foot, multi-leveled, multi-building residence came into view.

"Jeez!" Maeve's eyes widened. She pushed designer shades from her face to her forehead. "You call that a castle?"

"What would you call it?"

"Ginormous!"

"Ha!"

Victor's chest swelled with pride. It had taken him five years, two construction companies and seven different interior designers to complete the home of his dreams. The white stone and steel exterior gleamed in the sunlight and contrasted with the turquoise blue ocean below it. Horses lazily grazed in the distance. Palm and fruit trees dotted the landscape—coconut, banana, lemon, apple, avocado. It was an architectural masterpiece, a work of art and, outside of work, his greatest accomplishment. That it impressed someone of Maeve's caliber meant everything.

"Oh, my God, is that a chicken?"

Victor slowed to let the mother hen leading a row of

chicks pass. "Free range, organic," he explained. "Most of the food I and the staff eat is grown right here."

"Victor Cortez, you're full of surprises."

He wriggled his brows suggestively. "How do you Americans say it? You ain't seen nothin' yet."

They passed three one-bedroom guesthouses before reaching Victor's seven-bath, ten-bedroom open-air estate. Maeve was full of compliments regarding his home, exclaiming over each state-of-the-art this and luxurious that. Victor had spent millions having this estate built. Maeve's reaction made it worth every penny.

They reached the third-floor landing. "I had Hasina prepare two guest rooms. One has a mountain view, the other faces the ocean."

"What? No room with both?" Maeve mocked.

"Only mine."

He watched Maeve's throat move as she visibly swallowed.

"You'll see it later."

For once, she didn't argue. There was a first for everything. *Score one for me!*

"Considering you might be tired from traveling, I thought tonight we'd enjoy a simple dinner and perhaps a swim at sunset. The rest of the days can be as full or as relaxed as you'd like. The island holds much to see and do."

"It was a trek to get here. Simple sounds good. Also, I can see mountains in Chicago, so I'd love the room with the ocean view."

"Hasina will have your luggage delivered there. Would you like some time to rest, or freshen up? I'd love to give you a tour of the property but will totally understand if you'd rather unwind."

"I'm fascinated by how your place is designed and would love a tour. A quick shower and I'll be as good as new."

All kinds of shower comments came to mind, including him joining her in it, but he practiced gentlemanly decorum and refrained from saying them.

"Then meet me downstairs in, say, an hour?"

"I can meet you in half that."

"Perfect. Wear something casual and shoes for walking. A couple of the places I'd like you to see are only accessible on foot."

The look Maeve gave was unreadable. "The adventure begins."

"Indeed." He stepped forward and kissed her forehead. "I'm so glad you're here."

"Me, too."

Victor went downstairs and hung out near the first-floor landing. He didn't want Maeve to have to look for him in his massive spread. It was easy to get lost in there. Soon, Hasina joined him. She rolled a small tote behind her.

"What's that?"

She stopped directly in front of him and thrust the handle into his hand. "A light snack. Poor girl has arrived from a long tiring trip and you don't even offer a cool drink of water." She clucked and tsked as she chastised him. "Where are your manners?"

"Obviously misplaced. Thank you for your thoughtfulness."

"The bluff overlooking this place and all beyond it would be a perfect place to have refreshments. Leandro packed everything—utensils, napkins, water and a nice bottle of wine."

She glanced toward the staircase, then leaned in and whispered, "This one here, she special. Could be the one. Don't blow it."

Hasina winked, turned around and headed back to the kitchen before Victor could ask how she could possibly know anything about a woman she could have only glimpsed as he and Maeve had crossed the massive foyer and gone upstairs. Still, about a half hour later, as Maeve descended the stairs every inch a vision in white, he could do nothing but agree with his housekeeper and longtime member of the Cortez family. Wearing a flowy tee, shorts and high-top canvas sneakers, she looked very special. Victor had no plans to marry but if he did, Maeve looked like the woman who'd fit perfectly in his world, on his arm and in his bed.

"You look ravishing," he greeted with a brief kiss on the lips.

Maeve ducked and looked around. "Don't do that," she muttered, though the way she'd pressed her lips against his told him she didn't mean it.

"I'll do that and much more," he warned, inhaling her clean, freshly showered scent of citrus and flowers. "My house, my rules."

Maeve ran a flustered hand through her hair before pointing at the tote beside him. "What's that?"

Victor felt the question a distraction from the palpable sexual tension flowing between them. The thought pleased him immensely.

"Hasina thought that after such a long journey, you might be hungry. Her husband, Leandro, packed us a light lunch."

"That was very thoughtful of her."

"Hasina is one of the kindest, most thoughtful persons I've ever met. This household couldn't run without her."

"A husband and wife team runs our estate, too. Claude and Bernice have been in our family for decades. They knew me before I was born."

"Same here. You ready?"

"Absolutely."

They returned to the same Jeep that had carried them from the airport. Within minutes, they were traversing a two-lane roadway that spanned the circumference of his vast estate. He pointed out various gardens and structures of his fully sustainable organic farm, fish-filled lake and greenhouses along with a ten-hole golf course immaculately maintained, basketball and tennis courts, and a scenic tree-lined walking trail. Conversation centered around the thoughtful design, the stunning foliage and the sparkling water that surrounded them.

"This is truly paradise," Maeve said as the Jeep veered off the paved road onto one covered with gravel. "How did you find this land?"

"It's been in our family for a long time, purchased by my grandfather a few years after he migrated over from Jamaica in the mid-1900s. I spent my summers here and fell in love with nature, with the ocean and farming. A love my grandfather nourished and cherished because his son, my father, wanted nothing to do with the countryside where he'd grown up. He left for college, fell in love with the city and is Mr. Cosmopolitan to this day."

"You don't strike me as a country bumpkin."

"I'm no bumpkin. But contrary to what some may assume, I prefer the peace and quiet of open spaces like this to the hustle and bustle of the urban metropolis."

They reached an area on the side of the road just large enough for Victor to pull over and park. "This is as far as the Jeep can take us. We'll walk the rest of the way."

"Where are we going?"

"Heaven."

Maeve's expression made him laugh out loud. He leaned over and kissed her because, quite frankly, he couldn't go another second without fully tasting her lips. He got out of the Jeep, reached into the back for the food-laden tote and walked around to open Maeve's door. Taking her hand, he escorted them through a grove of trees that led to a set of stairs carved out of the mountain. The sky was a vibrant blue. The air was fresh. At this altitude, the clouds appeared to be close enough to touch.

"This feels magical," Maeve whispered.

He squeezed her hand. "It is."

They reached the top of the mountain. He turned to take in Maeve's reaction. Her eyes glistened. His heart leaped.

She gently pulled her hand from his and did a slow one-eighty, taking in the mountains, the ocean, the islands dotting the tranquil waters. Feeling like somewhat of an interloper, he opened the tote and busied himself removing the contents. He spread the blanket on the grass, set out the dishes and flatware, then removed a container of salad, another of blackened salmon and a cloth-wrapped basket of rolls. He'd just reached for the two cold bottles of alkaline water when he felt a pair of soft hands massaging his shoulders.

"Thanks for bringing me here."

He took a breath for control before rising to his full height of six feet four inches. "Thanks for appreciating the beauty as much as I do."

He kissed her forehead. Her cheek. Her lips. "And careful putting your hands on me. I might not be able to resist returning the favor."

"I might not want you to."

Her words provided all the encouragement he needed to do what he'd wanted to do since she got off the plane. Pulling her close, he wrapped his arms around her, covered her mouth with his and swiped her lips with his tongue. She opened them quickly, willingly, her own arms encircling his neck, her body pressing hard against his, her tongue seeking and scorching his mouth with its heat. A moan sounded within her throat, a sound of satisfaction that conveyed how he felt. That suddenly all was right with the world. That a missing piece had found its place and his life was complete. His hand crept toward her ass. He stopped himself before cupping its fullness, knowing that if he touched that globe of goodness, he might not be able to stop himself from going over the edge, from stripping them both and having his way with her. The thought of being sheathed in her warmth sent a rush of blood to his dick. With sheer will born from years of discipline—in sports, school, work—he pulled away.

"Let's eat."

What he really wanted to devour was wrapped in his arms. With a last quick kiss, however, he pulled them from around her and helped her settle on the blanket. But not before noting her dilated eyes, bruised lips and skin flushed with desire. He felt it, too. For the next week, he wanted nothing more than to explore that desire, and every inch of her body. He'd made grandiose plans for her stay, filled with fun and friends and parties and adventure. Those plans no longer mattered. He wanted Maeve all to himself.

"Are you going to join me?"

He adjusted himself in his canvas shorts. "Now that I can sit down, um, sure."

Her shy look away was endearing and, while not intending to, filled with promises of what was to come. As much as he wanted to, he wouldn't rush their inevitable joining. Wouldn't demand what in his heart he already knew was his. Victor's disbelief in successful relationships had placed a barrier over his heart. Slowly, with every word, kiss, gesture, Maeve was pushing past it.

Thirteen

Maeve should have felt conflicted. But all she felt was convinced. Convinced that Victor was everything she'd ever wanted in a man. That he wanted her as much as she wanted him and that tonight when he tried to finish what had started in a darkened country club hallway, she wouldn't resist. She knew in a way that went beyond logic that after this vacation, her life would never be the same. She shouldn't have any of these thoughts, feel any of these emotions. But she did.

To be sure, the conflict had been there. Fear, too. Conflict for all the obvious reasons. That he was opposing counsel in a suit against Eddington Enterprise. That for all intents and purposes, she'd be sleeping with the enemy. Then there was the feeling that happened whenever she saw him, even thought about him. They'd not even made love and already she felt the tugging of something that felt frighteningly close to the *L* word. Ridiculous, of course. Only in romance novels did people fall in love that quickly. Maeve felt happily-ever-afters mainly happened there, too. Unlike her parents, her best friend, Regina, her brother Desmond, Cayden and other successful couples she could name, lasting happiness had not occurred in her life. The time she'd tried, those years she'd made herself vulnerable and given herself over to Lionel completely, had been rewarded with his betrayal and ultimate rejection. The memories had faded over the past four years but the thought brought back the pain. The replay still stung. After his sudden marriage to a woman from another state whom Maeve had never heard of let alone met, she vowed she'd never put herself in such a position again. Since then, she'd dated cautiously and carefully, vetted potential suitors even for casual dalliances. There'd been good guys who were interested, like Cornelius and Matthias, guys who were faithful and predictable and safe. Then again, she'd thought the same about Lionel. He'd fit all those descriptions. Until he hadn't.

Feeling her careful mood start to slip, Maeve forced away yesterday and rose from the chair where she'd sat to slide on a pair of sparkly, strappy sandals. Victor had been the perfect host. As amazing as the day had been, it was tonight to which Maeve most looked forward. She crossed the room to the massive walk-in closet and over to the vanity where she'd laid out her jewelry, snapped on a thin diamond tennis bracelet to go with a set of single-strand drop earrings, her only other jewelry to complement the colorful maxi she'd chosen for tonight's dinner at sunset as Victor had described. With one last look in the mirror, she headed for the door and was almost there when her phone rang. Remembering Reign's earlier text, she hurried back to answer it.

"Hey, sis."

"Don't *hey sis* me. I've been waiting all day to hear from you!"

"You got my text."

"Are we serious right now? You're halfway on the other side of the world and I'm supposed to be okay with a simple message saying you arrived safely?"

Clearly, Reign was upset, yet Maeve couldn't keep the smile out of her voice. "I'm sorry."

"No, you're not."

"I am! It's been a full day. I was going to call you tomorrow."

"Well, now you don't have to. I'm here right now."

"And I'm headed to dinner."

"Not until you give me a quick update. How's it going? Is Victor still fine. Have you screwed him yet?"

"Reign!"

"Oh, my bad. Have the two of you had relations?"

"Now you sound like Grandma."

"Stay on subject, girl. You've got places to be, remember?"

"Okay, five minutes." Maeve walked out on the balcony overlooking the garden and ocean beyond. "To answer your questions, everything is fabulous. Victor's home is to die for and he is being the perfect host.

"No, we haven't…had relations."

"But you will."

"I don't know."

"Liar! How happy he's making you comes through the phone. Don't overthink things, Maeve. It's past time that you move on from old hurts and get fully back in the love game."

"I don't know what love has to do with it but I'm having a great time."

Maeve quickly filled in Reign on a day that, after their picnic atop a mountain, had included a trip into the heart of Puerto Limon and a history lesson on the area's colorful and somewhat controversial beginnings. They'd returned to Victor's estate, enjoyed a rousing game of tennis and a pleasant conversation over tea with Leandro and Hasina.

"They remind me of Claude and Bernice," Maeve finished. "It's my first day at this place and in his country but already I feel right at home."

"Hmm. I bet Victor has something to do with that homey feeling."

"Speaking of my handsome host, I'd best get downstairs. Give everyone a hug for me and please reassure the brothers that their sister is happy and safe."

"Were you eavesdropping on my conversation with them this morning?"

"No, but I know my brothers."

"I'll pass on your message and keep their search dogs at bay."

"I owe you one."

"Once back here, you'll owe me details, sister. I want to hear it *all*."

The smile on Maeve's face after speaking with Reign only widened when she went downstairs and laid eyes on Victor. He'd changed from the outfit worn earlier to a pair of black slacks and matching tunic.

Seeing her, he immediately walked over for a kiss. "You look amazing."

"Thank you."

"Our country is known for its incredible flora, but you put our most magnificent flower to shame."

Every compliment removed a link from the chain around her heart. But Maeve hid their effect behind sarcasm. "Pouring it on a little thick, aren't you?"

"Only speaking the truth, my love."

Maeve told herself he'd probably used that term of endearment on a million girls. And it probably helped remove the panties on them all, just as it most likely would do with her. Deciding not to keep fighting the inevitable, she vowed to enjoy the night.

Taking the arm he offered, she commented, "You look good, too."

"I try."

"Where's dinner?"

"Not far."

Moments later, Victor pulled out one of two chairs in the romantic setting that had been erected on pristine white sand on his private beach. Dinner was simple and delicious, not that later Maeve would remember what they ate, how it tasted or what they talked about. To celebrate her arrival, Victor uncorked a vintage bottle of Dom Pérignon's Reserve de L'Abbaye that tasted sublime. With each bubbly sip, Maeve lost her reserve and gained more nerve. It's the only explanation for how moments after arriving back at the house she ended up in Victor's suite, and in his bed.

They'd arrived back just after midnight. Exhaustion from the long journey had finally kicked in and, along with the liquor, caused Maeve's eyes to droop and yawns to escape as the two walked along the sand by moonlight. Victor noticed and insisted they head back to the house. Once there, they mounted the steps. He stopped at the door to her guest suite, gave her a chaste kiss good-night and continued down the hall to the master.

Maeve entered her room, showered and donned one of the lingerie she'd purchased for the trip. The sheer floor-length number was trimmed in lace with waist-high slits up both sides and a matching thong. She climbed onto a cloud-like mattress, closed her eyes and sought the sleep that less than an hour before felt ready to overtake her. She didn't know whether it was the shower that had revived her or the awareness of Victor's nearness. After several tortuous moments of tossing and turning, Maeve knew she needed a nightcap, and she knew said nightcap was likely enjoying a restful sleep just down the hall.

She eased out of bed and down the hall. A thrill of excitement raced through her at the boldness of her steps. Her actions were as crazy as they were out of character. In her mind, she heard both Reign and Regina cheering her on.

She quietly opened the door, then stood for several seconds as her eyes adjusted to the darkness. At the entrance of the L-shaped master suite was a sitting area. Maeve imagined Victor lying just around the corner, hard and probably naked, deep in sleep. How would he feel being awakened by her sliding into bed beside him?

Maeve didn't know, but she was about to find out.

She tiptoed around the corner and almost gasped out loud. Patio doors took up most of the wall. One was open, letting in the sound of waves and a cool night wind. Victor's

...were needed. ...the conversation. Maeve sat ...crotch, leaning down to let their lips get reacquainted. The kisses came hot and heavy. His hands felt like smelting iron as they moved up her arms, down her back before settling on her backside. He squeezed her cheeks. His tongue making slow, lazy circles with hers, even as her nipples, aching for touch, pebbled into hard buds against his chest. He groaned, pulled her up enough to take a nipple into his mouth. The feel of his wet tongue through the silky fabric sent a shot of desire straight through to her core. Wetness gushed between her legs. Her hips began grinding against the hardened sex now pulsating beneath her. His hands slid beneath the fabric and now were on her bare ass. He slid a finger between her cheeks, back and forth, up and down, as his tongue continued to assault her. Finally, she couldn't take anymore. She raised up and moved the fabric aside. His tip now rubbed against the lacy thong, the last barrier to complete and utter satisfaction. Of this, Maeve was sure. Victor hesitated only long enough to reach into the nightstand and pull out a condom. He rolled them over, put it on, then raised her leg and slid into her waiting wetness. She knew Victor would be an amazing lover. He didn't disappoint. The girth and length of him was powerful, the most exquisite torture. Her body adjusted and when it did, he quickened the pace, deepened the thrust, had her

illuminated by the light of the moon, moving as if into her
her body on fire and moving as if of its own accord. She approached the bed with caution, hoping not to wake him. She
was directly up on him before realizing he wasn't asleep.
but gazing at her. He'd been awake the whole time!

"Victor." The name came out in a breathless whisper.

He reached out a welcoming hand. "Come here."

She climbed onto the bed and immediately into his open
arms. No further words were spoken. None were

Instead, their bodies took over the

just above Victor's

Fourteen

In Chicago less than an hour and already Victor missed the warm rays of a Costa Rican sun. As the limo driver reached the entrance to a tall condominium building, Victor secured a wool scarf around his neck and pulled a matching cap over his close-cropped curls. He gave instructions to the driver regarding his luggage, then exited the vehicle and rushed up the walk.

"Victor?"

Instinctively, he turned around and immediately wished that he hadn't. It was Camela, wearing jeans, boots, a leather coat and a bright smile.

He retraced his steps beneath the black awning and met her at the sidewalk. "Hi, Camela."

"Hey, handsome!"

She leaned in for a hug. It took strength to keep her at arm's length. Thankfully, she played it off.

"I thought you went home for the holidays."

"I did."

She fixed him with a flirty look. "But you missed me so much you had to come back, right?"

Ignoring her comment, Victor asked his own question. "Do you live in the area?"

"Why? Want to come home with me?"

"Anything is possible."

"I was dropping off something at that building there." She pointed to another high-rise down the street.

"I see." Victor looked at his watch. "I'm headed to a meeting so…take care of yourself, okay?"

That his meeting was probably with the television or the shower meant that technically he hadn't lied.

He turned to walk away.

"You owe me a date!"

Victor grimaced. He owed her nothing. "Sorry, not this trip," he threw over his shoulder. With a backward wave of his hand, he continued into the building. After a quick and discreet stop at the security kiosk to reemphasize the importance of his privacy and not receiving unwanted guests, he continued to the elevator and his new home away from home.

Once inside, Victor went directly to the study, one of the rooms that had sold the house. He placed his briefcase on the table, fired up the electric fireplace and stood in front of it, trying to shake off both the cold and Camela's unexpected appearance, while glancing around at the architectural details of the two-bed, three-bath Lake Shore condo he'd purchased on a whim. He'd told his Realtor it was because he was tired of hotel living. When she'd pointed out that a short-term rental would have been a much easier and less expensive solution, he'd offered a totally out-of-the-box and off-the-top-of-his-head excuse about expanding his healthy portfolio to include real estate.

"In Chicago?"

"Yes."

"As in…Illinois."

Pause. Sigh. "Yes."

From the tone of this answer, she'd wisely stayed quiet after that and moved ahead with not only the purchase but the hiring of an interior decorator. With a flurry of video conference calls and less than two weeks' notice, the internationally known designer Sam Breedlove had well-earned her enormous salary. The furnishings were sensible yet sophisticated, a perfect complement to views of Lake Michigan from almost every room. He could already see him and Maeve enjoying a cup of java after a night of lovemaking, though he refused to let the possibility of her being the reason for the purchase cross his mind. Still, after picking up the phone with the full intention of calling his clients, specifically the Duberry heirs, and setting up a meeting, he found himself scrolling the contacts and tapping on the number under another name.

Maeve picked up on the second ring. "Hello?"

"What are you wearing?"

"Hold on." Victor heard the sound of papers being shuffled followed by a soft thud that signaled the closing of a door. "No, you did not just ask me that tired question."

Hearing a woman's laughter over the phone should not make a man this happy. But it did.

"Yes, I asked that…and your coochie tingled just a little bit, didn't it?"

"You wish it had."

"No, you wish I were there to make it tingle even more."

Both of them laughed because they knew it was true.

Victor leaned back in the chair and adjusted his jeans to give his rapidly hardening member a bit more room. Then he placed his bare size fifteens on the study's coffee table as if instead of talking to clients and preparing legal arguments, he had all the gab time in the world.

"Can I be honest with you about something?"

"An honest attorney?" Maeve replied. "Not sure it's possible."

"Ha!" Her self-depreciating humor was adorable. He gave himself a bit more room.

"When I'm talking to you," he continued, his voice low and silky, "sometimes my dick gets hard."

Several seconds of silence followed.

And then several more.

He heard Maeve clear her throat before asking, quite unexpectedly, "Is it hard now?"

"Damn." Victor shifted in his seat. He reached down and casually stroked his burgeoning manhood. "Hard as a rock. My coffee table is glass. I could probably take the tip of my shaft and etch my name on it."

"Oh, my gosh!" Maeve laughed unabashedly now. "That I would like to see."

"Good. Come on over."

"You know that's not possible."

"Why not?"

"You ask that question way too often. Are you forgetting the very detailed conversation we had before leaving Costa Rica, the one about ending our intimate connection and casual interactions until after this case was done?"

"I remember. I still want you to come over, and before you decline me for the second time in as many minutes, there's something you should know."

"What?"

"I'm not at the Ritz."

"Really? Where are you staying?"

"A nice little condo on Lake Shore Drive. Private. Discreet. I've already paid off security. I could send a car over once your work day is over and have dinner delivered."

"That sounds very tempting, but I must decline."

"Maeve, it's just dinner."

"With each other as dessert."

"Doesn't that sound delicious?"

"Mouthwatering. Which is why it absolutely cannot happen. Hold on a sec, Victor. Yes?"

Victor heard muffled voices. Maeve returned to the phone.

"Sorry, but I have to go now. With our case coming up on the docket quickly, I doubt I'll have time to chat again before then."

"But Maeve, wait—"

"Take care of yourself." Her near-whispered ending set his nerves on edge. He'd been attracted to Maeve from the moment he spotted her at that party on the college campus all those years ago. Knowing how she felt, the abandoned way she made love, made him want her even more now.

Too bad. Wasn't happening. At least not for another week.

With the case in mind, Victor tabled the wishful-thinking, and after retrieving a cold water from the state-of-the-art kitchen, grabbed his tablet from the bedroom and got down to business. His first call was to Hubert III, a client who was proving to be as hard to peg as he was hard to reach. Fortunately, today, he picked up right away.

"Mr. Cortez! Happy New Year!"

"Sounds like yours was happy. Are you still celebrating?"

"As a matter of fact, I am. One of my artists just got signed to a major record label. It was a seven-figure deal."

Victor began to take notes. "Artists? I didn't know you were in the music business."

"I dabble around."

"Are you a producer?"

"More like a manager, or consultant. I wear different hats."

"Interesting. I called to let you know I'm back in town and that we should meet ASAP, you and I, along with your sisters."

"What do we need to meet for?"

Victor frowned as he stood and walked to a window overlooking a jogging path and small park. "Regarding a pesky little matter called a lawsuit against Eddington Enterprise, the reason I'm in the Midwest."

"I hired you to handle that."

"Which would be easier if reaching you weren't such a problem."

"I told you I'd be gone for the holidays."

"Yes, you did." In an effort to stay calm and not react, Victor pinched the bridge of his nose. "Out of the country, but exactly where I don't recall. Did you have a good time?"

"The best."

"Did your sisters go, too? I reached out to them as well and heard nothing back."

"They spent the holidays in London, with our mom."

"Your mom." Victor flipped pages on his tablet. "Daphne, correct? She lives there full-time?"

"For the past two years."

"What's her full name?"

"Why all the questions about my mother?"

"Because she was married to your dad at the time your grandmother's will was drawn up. It's standard protocol to gather as much information as I can on all the players involved so that once in the judge's chamber, I don't get hit with surprises. I don't want anything to get in the way of you receiving those stolen millions as quickly as possible."

These words loosened Hubert's tongue. "Daphne Collins."

"Collins? She's remarried?"

"You're a smart guy."

And you're a smart-ass. "What's her husband's name?"

"Jeffrey."

"Do you know his occupation?"

"Nope."

"What about your mom? Does she work?"

Hubert found this question extremely funny. "Not a day in her life."

"Alright, then." Victor was ready for this conversation, and the case, to be over. "Is it possible to meet with the three of you tomorrow for lunch, in downtown Chicago, say around twelve thirty, one o'clock. It's very important."

"My sisters aren't here. They're back at school in DC."

"Not a problem. I'll get in touch with them after this phone call and set up a video conference instead. Once I get their class schedule, I'll get back with you regarding the time."

"Yeah, well, let me know ASAP. I'm a busy man."

"Thanks for that information, Hubert. I'll keep it in mind."

Victor contacted the twins, who were much more cordial than their brother had been. He texted the meeting time to Hubert, then emailed his secretary. For the rest of the evening, Victor scoured the internet for all he could find on Hubert's mother, Daphne, and anything he may have missed on Hubert Jr. and their children. He learned that Daphne's given name was Everett and that she'd grown up in Washington DC's tony Prince George's County, the daughter of a socialite and a NASA engineer. She'd attended Howard University and married Hubert right out of college. He knew from past research that Hubert Jr. had graduated from Howard with a master's in political science and had dabbled in real estate, finance and politics before his untimely death. Mostly, it appeared that he'd specialized in running his mother Lillian Duberry's estate, along with her substantial financial portfolio. Victor had to admit he'd done a pretty good job.

From the stories he read and pictures he found, Daphne seemed to be doing well. Her current husband, referred to as Sir Jeffrey online, had obscure but royal ties to Luxembourg and what looked to be a decorated military background. There were photos of the two alongside England's duchess and prince, and ones of him decked out in ceremonial and polo garb. At first glance, it would appear Daphne would have no need for Mrs. Duberry's money. But Victor had been an attorney long enough to know that things were seldom as they appeared.

The sisters were sophomores majoring in music and health education and, from what he gleaned from their social media, were typical young adults trying to live their best lives.

He couldn't say the same for Hubert, III. The kid had graduated high school three years ago and spent less than a year at his parents' alma mater before dropping out for reasons unknown.

"Probably to manage rappers," Victor mumbled aloud as he clicked on various pictures found on Hubert's social media. Most were of him in an entourage, mean-mugging the camera, flashing fancy jewelry and wads of cash and surrounded by scantily clad women. On one hand, these were the perfectly believable antics of a spoiled rich kid. On the other, they were of a man with more money than he knew how to spend. Where was he getting it? Not from the trust, which had been thoughtfully established by Hubert Jr. before he died. It provided for his children's education, a sensible monthly stipend and larger payoffs at the ages of thirty, forty and fifty years old.

The more he saw, the less confident he felt about representing Hubert III specifically or winning the case. He'd taken it on as a favor to Cornelius, the former friend and classmate who'd recused himself, citing a conflict of interest. He'd thought the conflict was Cornelius's feelings for Maeve. Instead, was it possibly being in cahoots with Daphne or Hubert to help spend Mrs. Duberry's money? Victor hated having such thoughts regarding a friend, but money made folk do strange things. He went to bed feeling troubled. Something didn't add up. He didn't know what about the information was making him uncomfortable, but he was determined to find out.

As much as the case weighed on him, something else wasn't right. Maeve wasn't where she belonged—in his bed. He planned to fix that, too, and soon.

Fifteen

"**Y**ou did it."

On January 2, when Reign picked up Maeve from the private landing strip, because she'd insisted, those were the first words that had come out of her mouth.

"Did what?" had been Maeve's ridiculous comeback.

"Yeah, you slept with him. You're all but glowing, sis."

That had been the beginning of a two-hour interrogation. Reign didn't have to press too hard. Maeve had been only too willing to relive the amazing time she'd enjoyed with Victor by sharing the delicious details with her sister. How they'd yachted and zip-lined and Jet-Skied and swam naked at midnight. How she'd dined with Victor's father, Arly, and the stunning wife not much older than his son. How on New Year's Eve there had indeed been fireworks, both outdoors and in the bedroom. So, no, Maeve hadn't denied that she and Victor had been intimate. That she'd been sexed to within an inch of eternity was probably written all over her face.

"I did."

Reign squealed, "Yes," and pumped her fist in the air.

"Look, cheerleader, it's not like I made a three-pointer, okay?"

"No, but he probably did." Reign laughed at her attempt at a joke.

"No games involved. It just…happened." And Maeve had been second-guessing the decision ever since.

"And I'm glad it did. You stay locked up in your lonely comfort zone—" Reign made air quotes "—feeling totally uncomfortable."

Maeve began to object.

"Don't even go there and try and deny it. Sure, you can go out with a date every night but how many of those guys do you really want to be with more than Victor?"

Absolutely no one. The energy behind the statement was so electric Maeve didn't even have to say it aloud.

"I thought so." They reached Maeve's home on the grounds of the Estate. Reign popped her trunk, then hooked her arm with Maeve's as they wheeled luggage to the wrought iron and beveled glass double front doors. "So tell me," she whispered, in that conspiratorial tone that only sisters can share, "is he as good in bed as he looks?"

Maeve smiled, resting a shoulder on the door jamb. "Better, Reign," she finally said with a sigh. "Much better than that. It wasn't only the best sex I've ever had, it's the best I'll experience in this lifetime."

Maeve pressed Save on the document she'd been typing in, then pushed away from her desk. She stood, stretched and reached for a mug of coffee, her third that morning. Before ten o'clock. She'd been hard at work since seven that morning, hoping to wrap up the argument she'd present in Judge Keller's chambers next week. Sipping her vanilla caramel-laced, espresso-boosted cup of energy, she walked over to the large windows that covered most of her office's back wall. Having that much natural light was one of the room's best features. Her eyes swept the landscape. Tall verdant pines, their needles dusted from last night's mild snow, stood in contrast to the majestic oak, ash and maples whose branches had long ago shed their colorful fall leaves and now stretched hard and naked toward the sky. The snow-covered ground and cloudy light gray skies bathed the surroundings in winter white serenity, totally opposite of how Maeve felt on the inside. Between a vague uncertainty about the upcoming trial's outcome, and near-constant thoughts of Victor, her stomach stayed in knots.

A light tap on her door was followed by the sound of it opening. "Maeve, you got a minute?"

She turned around. "Sure, Raymond. Come on in."

Bypassing her desk, she walked to a small round table surrounded by four leather, brass-studded ivory chairs. A vase containing a winter bouquet of vibrant blue delphinium, huge yellow roses and fragrant white oriental lilies sat on a brass plate adorning the middle of the smoky-colored glass top. She reached for a coaster, set her mug down on it and took a seat. Raymond Zewinksy followed suit, his bulky frame barely contained in the chair. An ex-wrestling mathematical genius who looked more like a bodyguard than an accountant, with shocking red hair and devilish green eyes, he was one of the best things that had ever happened to Eddington Enterprise.

"I know the holidays are over, but I hope you're bringing me good tidings of great joy."

"Could be." He set a folder on the desk. So deep in thoughts about Victor's magic wand, she hadn't even noticed Raymond had been carrying a folder. He flipped it open and slid a single sheet of paper across the table.

"What's this?"

"That's what I'm trying to figure out. We brought in a forensic accountant to scour the Duberry records, see if there was possibly anything we'd missed. Buried deep within the confines of her largest investment portfolio was the trust you see in front of you."

Maeve picked up the sheet of paper. "Stone Mountain Fiduciary." Her brows knit. "Stone Mountain, Georgia?"

Raymond shrugged.

"Isn't Hubert's ex-wife from Atlanta?" Maeve walked over to her desk and retrieved a small MacBook. She returned to her seat, fired it up and typed Daphne Everett-Duberry into the search engine.

"Hubert as in the kid's late father?" Raymond asked.

"Um-hmm."

"Good question. I don't know."

"Looks like the ex–Mrs. Everett-Duberry is now Mrs. Daphne Collins." Maeve clicked on a few more links, then tapped the *images* on the search engine. A smiling Daphne stood next to a distinguished-looking gentleman with blond hair and blue eyes who had an arm possessively around her.

"Lots of pictures from Europe, especially London. I wonder if this new husband is English."

"I wonder if she's the one who was somehow able to set up a trust within a trust and move money over there without us knowing."

"How could that happen?"

"If someone wanted to be devious enough, there are ways. Complicated, intricate, but possible."

"Wouldn't that require help from someone working on the inside, from our company?"

Raymond huffed, picked up his mug and took a long sip. "Yes, it does, and I'm afraid that's a possibility."

"Explain."

"Remember Louis, the mathematical and computer whiz kid we hired two years back?"

"Mr. MIT? Who could forget? He left rather quickly, as I recall."

"Yeah, family emergency is what he told us."

"You think it could be more? You think he could have…"

The sentence died as Maeve watched Raymond's green eyes darken to the color of emeralds. She reached toward a phone on a credenza beyond her and tapped the speaker button.

"Derrick, it's Maeve."

At corporate, her father was addressed by his name. At home, he became Daddy once again.

"What's up, Maeve?"

"Do you have a minute to come to my office?"

"Not really."

"I think you need to carve out about ten minutes. It's regarding the Duberrys."

"Be right there."

Ten minutes after Derrick arrived, Desmond and Jake were called in, too. Within the hour, two more members of the finance department had been summoned, along with the expert in forensic accounting who'd discovered the obscure account. By the end of the week, more discoveries had been made, information that could change the trajectory of the court case or cause it to be withdrawn altogether. Either way, Maeve knew there was no way they could proceed on schedule. She'd have to contact Judge Keller and request a delay. First, there was someone else she needed to call. Her fingers had been itching to call Victor all week. She was glad to finally have a legitimate reason.

She waited until the end of the day when encased in the privacy of her car. Tapping the Bluetooth, she tapped his name in her contact list.

"About time you called."

His greeting took her aback and at the same time made her smile. A pretty darn good week just got a whole lot better.

"The phone works both ways."

"True, but during our last conversation, you were quick to remind me that talking to you about anything other than the case was not acceptable."

"You don't strike me as a man who only does what's expected."

"You don't strike me as a woman who likes to break rules."

"Sounds like there's more that both of us need to get to know about the other."

"Is that why you're calling after work hours on a Friday? Because you'd like to come over and…get to know me better?"

The drop in his voice—both timbre and tone—sent squiggles straight to Maeve's love box.

"I definitely want us to meet, but before you get excited you should know that it's about the case."

"What about it?"

"I'm going to contact the judge on Monday and request a delay."

"Why?"

"Because of some new information revealed from a forensic accountant's thorough review of the Duberry records, facts that you need to know about before they're entered as new evidence."

"What did he find?"

"An obscure trust account linked to Hubert Jr.'s ex-wife."

"And the mother of my clients."

"Bingo. Are you free to meet tonight? I could come where you are and arrange to have dinner delivered."

"That sounds good. Wait, on second thought, perhaps we should meet somewhere else."

"Look, even though this meeting is strictly business, I'd rather it happen in the privacy of your home. I'd invite you to the Estates, but to get here you'd have to drive through a town that is much too small to guarantee your arrival would go unnoticed. At this critical juncture in the case, I don't want there to be any appearance of impropriety."

At that word, a memory flashed before Maeve's eyes—her legs in the air and Victor's head lodged between them.

"I'm not worried about that. I had an unfortunate run-in the day I arrived back here."

Maeve forced her mind back to the present. "With whom?"

"Camela."

"Oh." Maeve switched into the left-hand turn lane and peered at her windshield with narrowed eyes. *Is that snow?*

"Where'd you see her?"

"Unfortunately, right in front of my building. I played if off as being here for a meeting, but she's called Cornelius to try and ascertain my whereabouts."

"Told you Chicago was a small town."

"Too small for me."

"Don't tell me she lives there."

"No. She was dropping off something at a high-rise down the street. Her car was parked closer to my building."

"Then I agree that meeting there isn't the best idea. It's important, though, that I see you this weekend. For work," she emphasized.

"Should I meet you at the club? I haven't leased a car yet, but I could have a service drive me over. And since it's the weekend, I could spend the night at your place."

Maeve figured that anywhere near her town was the last place Victor needed to be. Her willpower couldn't take it. In all likelihood, she'd blink her eyes and find him in her bed.

"Text me your address. I'll find someplace for us to meet, away from the city, off the beaten path."

"Should I pack an overnight bag?"

"No, but you might want your briefcase and computer. I'll be by in an hour."

"I'll be ready."

Maeve stopped by her place only long enough to change out of her suit and into a comfortable pair of jeans, flat boots, a bulky sweater and her favorite oversize down coat. She pulled her hair into a ponytail, slid on a knit cap and placed the matching gloves in her coat pockets. Returning to her car, she sent a text to her dad and one to Reign before heading up the hill to her father's ten-car garage, where she exchanged her sporty Aston for a less conspicuous and more practical SUV. Finally, after engaging her Bluetooth, she checked the weather forecast. Even though the flurries she'd seen on the way home seemed to be increasing, there was only a 20-percent chance that they'd get any real precipitation. Then she tapped on directions for the out-of-the-way, überexclusive restaurant she'd gone to only once before, even as she forced down the memory of why she'd gone there. Lionel. The night he proposed. Then she remembered another moment, the one only months later where she found out Lionel had gotten married to his conveniently pregnant high-society side chick. The feeling of melancholy that swept over her was soon replaced by one of anger and resolve. No better way to put that memory behind her than to dine at the same spot with Victor, a man with the kind of lovemaking skills to make any woman forget about any other relationship, past or present. The fireworks that had exploded on New Year's Eve had made her forget her own name.

For a split second, she was tempted to return to her house and pack an overnight bag. Just as quickly, she reminded herself—business only. They'd discuss business over dinner and return to Chicago. No need for extra clothing. When she went to bed that night, Maeve determined, it would be in her own. Alone.

Sixteen

At a little past seven o'clock, Victor stood at the window, watching a light sprinkling of snowflakes dance against his view on the seventeenth floor. His nearby phone vibrated. He strolled over, picked it up and tapped its face to read Maeve's text.

I'm here, in front of the coffee shop around the corner.

Her obviously suspicious nature made him smile. She was probably thinking about his unexpected meeting with Camela. Walking into his bedroom, he considered the odds that his annoying anniversary date would be on his exact block at the precise moment his limo dropped him off. Probably a million to one.

What were the chances he'd talk Maeve into spending the night with him? Twice as great, most likely.

He slipped into the full-length leather coat he'd just purchased and grabbed his briefcase from off the dining room table. He was almost to the door when he thought to retrieve his phone charger, along with the Chicago Bears skullcap he'd purchased at the airport and worn that afternoon. With a last look around the place he was still getting used to calling home, he closed the door and locked it.

The elevator was empty. The lobby, too. A casual glance around as he headed toward the corner coffee shop took in a bare street. The weather, most likely. The wind off Lake

Michigan was ice-cold, felt like needles going right through the protective leather around him, the cashmere sweater he wore and into his skin. He turned the corner, saw taillights on a gray-colored SUV and hurried over. After a quick peek inside, he opened the door and was welcomed by a blast of warmth and the sounds of Lauren Hill.

"Nice," he said, rubbing his hands together and bobbing his head to the beat. "*The Miseducation*. A classic."

"One of my favorites."

"Mine, too." Maeve eased into the night's light traffic. "Cold enough for you?"

"I don't know how you guys live here."

"You get used to it, I guess."

"That frigid air? The ice and snow? Never." He leaned forward for a better look out the window. "Good thing that stuff's not sticking."

"I checked the forecast. It'll taper off shortly. The temps will drop around midnight but we're good."

"Where are we going?"

"A little place called Cook, about ninety minutes outside of town."

"What type of food do they...cook?"

Maeve laughed. "The chef has Greek and Turkish roots so while the menu boasts American cuisine, other dishes are definitely influenced by the food in those countries. I've only eaten there once before but I think you'll like it."

"I haven't eaten since lunch so they could serve a peanut butter sandwich and I'd give them five stars."

The small talk continued as they hit the interstate then veered off on to a two-lane road about twenty miles outside of Chicago.

"It's snowing harder up here," he observed.

Maeve nodded as she turned on the windshield wipers. "Yeah, it's picking up a little bit. Plus, I believe this is a county road. Probably takes those workers a little longer to clear it than the highways and interstates. Don't worry, though. Cook is a well-known restaurant within a quaint and popular hotel. It's always booked. They'll make sure the roads are okay."

"Did you say hotel?"

"Don't get any ideas. I'll have us back home before midnight."

Even as she said that, the snow began to fall harder.

Victor peered out the window. "You sure about that?"

"Positive. It's specifically why I chose to drive this car. It's got snow tires and front-wheel drive."

"What does that mean?"

"It means there's no chance of us getting stuck in these mountains." She patted the dash. "This baby will get us home."

They reached Hotel Bouvó without incident and were soon seated near a roaring wood fireplace, the restaurant's focal point located in the center of the room. The sommelier delivered a complimentary bottle of robust red wine, further warming the space. After a cheery server arrived with their appetizers, classic Greek salads and tasty mini skewers of lamb served with spiced pita bread, Maeve steered the conversation toward business.

"I think we've located the missing money, or at least where it was directed from its initial account."

Victor's raised brow was the only response. He continued chewing his food.

"A trust called Stone Mountain was discovered buried deep within the portfolio's records. Stone Mountain is a town located in Georgia."

Victor stopped eating. "Where Daphne Collins used to live."

"You know about her?"

"I've done my research."

"This case isn't making sense to you, either. That's why you're investigating."

"I always work to know as much as I can about my clients."

"Fair enough. We couldn't get access to the trust directly but know that at least ten million dollars, maybe more, was transferred there out of one of Mrs. Duberry's accounts."

"Wouldn't that have to involve one of your employees?"

Maeve reached for her glass of wine and sat back. "Possibly, but it would also require Hubert's willing participation and Daphne's forged signature."

"Not necessarily. Your employee could have forged the signature without the help of any member of the Duberry family." He watched Maeve's cool expression as she processed those words.

"Have you questioned your employees?"

"No."

She'd answered too quickly. Victor was sure there was more that she wasn't telling. The revelation also gave him another consideration. That his client could have been set up and was telling the truth all along.

"Why not?"

Maeve began eating again. "This is a very recent development. There is a lot to look into, which is why I'm informing you about the discovery."

Victor pulled out his phone. "The name of the employee who signed off on the transfer should be documented. I'll need that information."

"We'll turn over names and other documentation as they become relevant."

"I'd say a transfer within your system to an account outside it, presumably without Mrs. Duberry's permission, makes this very relevant."

"I'm not going to withhold anything from you, Counselor. Just want to make sure no one is questioned unfairly. The transaction trail is circuitous and murky. Unraveling it will take more time. I'm going to have to request another delay from the judge."

"She won't be too happy."

"I don't see how she can refuse it given the potential impact of what's been found out."

"Like the realization that my clients are innocent?"

"Like the money trail leads straight to Hubert Duberry the Third's and/or his mother's front door."

"I'll need you to turn over everything you intend to present as evidence."

Maeve outwardly bristled. Inwardly, Victor smiled. He loved getting under her skin almost as much as he loved getting on top of it.

"As I said, I'll turn over all relevant information. If I had planned to do otherwise, I wouldn't have requested this meeting."

"Not that I'll need all of what you have to beat you, just that it would only be fair."

"I'll give it to you. Those bedroom moves are mesmerizing. But when it comes to the courtroom, I'll definitely bring my A game."

"You'll need it."

Maeve's smile ran away as she leaned forward. "The best possible thing you could do is underestimate me."

"Is that right?" he asked, leaning close and feeling testy as well. Until her tempting lips distracted him and he pressed his own against them.

Maeve opened her mouth to object but looking beyond him clamped it shut. Right after, the reason why stopped next to their table. Their server, a tall man wearing a starched white shirt, black trousers and a bright smile, immediately lightened the mood.

"Ms. Eddington, Mr. Cortez, how's everything so far?"

"Excellent," Maeve answered, directing all the flirtatiousness Victor wanted to feel on to the now blushing waiter. "And please, call me Maeve."

"And me, Victor," he intoned with a scowl and extra

bass in his voice, breaking up the mutual admiration happening across the table.

"Yes, um, sir. May I offer the night's special…"

Maeve and Victor's "discussion" was sidetracked by some of the most delicious food Victor had ever tasted. Considering how extensively he'd traveled, that was saying a lot. The two opted for different entrées to sample the other's choice. Good move. Maeve's lobster, slathered with brown butter atop a bed of risotto was as decadent as Victor's thoughts about Maeve, his grilled rib eye as spicy as their last time in bed. The food was enough of a distraction for a temporary truce between the feisty lawyers as conversation drifted from winning cases to delicious cuisine. Victor plied Maeve with stories of various restaurants he'd visited around the world, which stoked her sense of adventure. Her stories about family settled around him like a wool blanket as he tried to imagine growing up in such a close-knit clan. By the time dessert menus were offered, laughter had replaced their snarling and Victor was reminded just how delightful he found Maeve's company, and how he definitely wanted to enjoy more of it.

"Of course, our traditional and popular baklava dessert is highly recommended," the waiter told them after a busboy had cleared their plates. "But if I may suggest that on a wintery night like this, the chef's rather unique take on the lava cake, one that involves a sinful amount of amaretto and chocolate liqueur, would be a perfect way to end the evening."

Victor raised a brow to Maeve who placed a hand on her stomach. "It sounds amazing, but I don't think I could eat another bite. What about you, Victor?"

"You're looking at a man who never turns down chocolate, but it's no fun to eat sweets alone."

"I could have the order sent up to your room," the waiter suggested. "Each suite has a mini fridge already stocked with a variety of beverages, but I could include a pitcher of iced coffee if you'd prefer."

"Oh, no, we only came for dinner. We're not spending the night."

The waiter's expression wavered between somber and surprise. "I think you might not have a choice."

"What do you mean?" Maeve demanded.

"As of a half an hour ago, Highway 9 was closed."

"Why didn't you tell us? How were we not somehow informed?"

"I'm sorry," the young man stuttered. "I just assumed—"

"Something you should never do!" Maeve whipped out her phone. "I'm sure there is a service who can get through to get us."

She tapped the phone's face to pull up a browser. "What, no internet, either?"

Out of the corner of his eye, Victor saw a middle-aged man approach, his title made clear by the starched white hat and jacket he wore.

"Good evening, Ms. Eddington," he said, smiling, his voice filled with warmth. "My name is Chef Kai. It is a pleasure seeing you again. I hope you found your meal most enjoyable."

Maeve continued to tap and swipe her phone. Victor answered instead. "She's trying to get a signal," he explained, extending his hand. "I'm Victor Cortez. The food was amazing."

Kai gave a slight bow. "Thank you, sir."

"Why weren't we told about the snowstorm?" Maeve interrupted. "That in staying for dinner, we risked not being able to return home."

"My sincerest apologies, Ms. Eddington. An announcement was made earlier in the evening, obviously before you arrived. Most of those dining are hotel guests and those who aren't booked rooms once the snowfall increased.

However, I'll be more than happy to secure a suite if one remains, complements of Cook."

"Mr. Cortez and I are here on a business meeting," Maeve snapped. "We'll need two rooms."

Kai nodded. "We'll do our best to accommodate your needs."

Ten minutes later, Kai returned. "I have good news and bad news," he said, looking from Maeve to Victor and back. "The good news is that we can accommodate you."

"And the bad news?" Maeve asked.

"We only have one suite remaining."

Maeve looked peeved. Victor was thrilled. His Friday night had just gotten better, and so had his liking for snow.

Seventeen

Victor and Maeve reached the suite, a classically decorated set of rooms with beauty totally lost on Maeve. She tossed her leather tote on the couch and flopped down in defeat.

"I can't believe how off the weather report was, or that they've closed the roads already." She eyed Victor, who looked cool, calm and somewhat smug as he tapped his phone. That shouldn't have perturbed her. The weather wasn't his fault. But his being so unbothered when her body was aching for him, causing her to want to pull out her hair, got on one of the last of the few nerves she had left.

"What are you doing?"

Victor barely reacted to her chaffing tone. "Checking out our options."

He walked to the window.

"You've got service?"

"Satellite phone."

"Well, why didn't you say so earlier? We could have called someone and perhaps been halfway home."

"That wasn't possible."

"How do you know?"

"I checked the internet."

"When?"

"When you were showing very bad behavior to a chef who didn't deserve it."

His comment shoved the sarcastic response Maeve was about to deliver back down her throat. Victor was right. Kai had been gracious and she'd been a jerk. She owed him an apology. Victor, too.

"I apologize for reacting out of frustration. What's happening is no one's fault."

"I can think of worse things than being stuck in a five-star hotel with an amazing woman."

"Have you forgotten we're scheduled to see the judge next week?"

"Not if the snow keeps coming down like this."

Maeve joined him at the window and beheld a winter wonderland. "This looks like a frickin' blizzard."

"I still might be able to get us out of here. I have a friend who might be able to help."

"How? By controlling the snow?"

Victor's smiled could have melted the ice off the windows. "That's not a bad idea. He owns a helicopter company and might have a partnering company here. If there is a helicopter landing pad nearby, we can potentially be lifted out."

Maeve's phone rang. Her eyes brightened. "We've got service!" She raced over and retrieved the phone from her tote. Victor waved as he left the room for the hotel lobby. Looking at the caller ID, her smile waned. Instead of Reign, the only person she'd told about dinner with Victor, it was Mona.

"Hey, Mom."

"Maeve! Thank goodness you finally answered. I've been trying to reach you."

"I had a business meeting at Hotel Bouvó. The service went down."

"You went all the way out there? In this weather?"

"It wasn't snowing that bad when I left Chicago."

"It caught everyone off guard. Came out of nowhere. They've just issued a winter storm warning."

"Oh, no! For how long?" Maeve tried to keep the panic

out of her voice, but staying away from Victor for one night was already impossible, let alone two.

"The next twenty-four to forty-eight hours. Don't stress about it, dear. That's a beautiful hotel. Treat this like an impromptu vacation."

"I don't have time for a vacation. I've got a case… I've got work to do."

"You don't have your computer?"

"Yes, but—"

"No buts. Work from there. Not tonight, though, darling. You sound as tight as a drum. Have a bottle of wine brought up to the room and take a long relaxing soak. You'll feel better tomorrow."

"Why were you trying to reach me?"

"It can wait."

"Mom…"

"Just some Point gossip. No big deal. I'll give the family an update so they don't worry. Keep me posted on when the road is cleared and you're on your way home."

"Will do."

Maeve ended the call and looked around. Really, the room was just way too romantic. The fireplace. Homey atmosphere. Big inviting bed. One look at the turquoise blue spread and she was back in Costa Rica with Victor, their hot bodies entwined in brash desire before being cooled by the open patio door's ocean breeze. She rushed to the window to turn off the memory. Big flakes of fluffy white snow brought her back to the Midwest. A knock on the door brought her back to reality. Had Victor forgotten his key?

Maeve crossed over and looked through the keyhole. It was a hotel employee holding a gift box. She unlocked the door. "Yes?"

"Ms. Eddington, this is for you."

"I don't think so. No one knows I'm here."

"It's from the hotel. A few amenities for our guests. We

know some of you didn't plan to spend the night and thought this gift box would help."

Maeve reached for it just as the elevator dinged and Victor strolled out. "I'll take that."

He reached into his pocket and pulled out a bill. "Thanks."

Continuing on to the table, he set down the box. Maeve followed him over. "What is it?"

Together, they checked out the contents: a bottle of wine, bottles of water, gourmet snacks, toiletries, candles.

"That was thoughtful," she said.

"I think so." Victor read the wine bottle label. "Would you like a glass?"

Maeve shook her head. "I'm good." She figured she was about one sip of wine away from jumping Victor's bones. Best to keep a clear head.

He walked over to the fireplace and, after a quick glance at the mantel, turned on the switch.

"Do we really need that?" Maeve asked.

Victor shrugged. "Looks nice."

"Fine. I'm going to check a few emails, take a shower and go to bed. Are there extra linens for the couch or should I have them bring some up?"

Victor's look was worth a thousand words. "The couch? Woman, I've never slept on a couch in my life."

"First time for everything," Maeve huffed before turning around and flouncing off to work at the desk in the bedroom.

His low-throated laugh was as irritating as it was sexy. It was all she could do not to try to slam the door shut. But she didn't. She was twenty-eight, not sixteen. Instead, she took a breath, pulled out a set of folders and her tablet, and tried to concentrate on the case.

Impossible. Especially with Victor now happily whistling in the other room. She wished for headphones but hers were unfortunately in the glove compartment of her car, not the family vehicle parked in the garage downstairs.

She sat back, tapping her fingers on the mouse as she

looked out the window. Freezing temperatures aside, Maeve loved this time of year. The snow made everything look clean and beautiful. Weather like this forced the world to slow down, take a breath. Any other time with any other person, she would have relished the setting, especially the fireplace. She'd loved them ever since believing that the chimney was how Santa came bearing gifts. Just beyond the door was another present to unwrap and play with, a gift named Victor. A real-life boy toy that was more off-limits than the apple in the world's first garden. The handsome devil himself had tried to warn her about the weather. But little miss know-it-all had to act like, well, like she knew it all. Snippets of the conversation they'd had as she drove to the hotel drifted through her mind.

I checked the forecast. It'll taper off shortly. The temps will drop around midnight but we're good.

It's snowing harder up here. That astute observation should have given her a clue. She'd been all too ready to ease his anxiety.

Yeah, it's picking up a little bit. Plus, I believe this is a county road. Probably takes those workers a little longer to clear it than the highways and interstates. Don't worry, though. Cook is a well-known restaurant within a quaint and popular hotel. It's always booked. They'll make sure the roads are okay.

Maeve had been so confident, so sure that the weather would stay mild and the roads, safe. Now, in this moment, all she felt was danger. Determined to get her mind off Victor, she pulled out the folder from accounting, the one with all the information on Louis Guitterez and had just begun researching his present whereabouts when the room went black.

Maeve froze, her hand hovering over the computer mouse. "What just happened?"

"I think it's the power. My phone just switched back from Wi-Fi to satellite. Electricity must be out." There was a pause before she heard Victor mumble to himself yet with a voice loud enough that she overhead him, "Looks like we're going to have candlelight, after all."

Maeve bit back a forlorn moan. It was hard enough controlling herself in broad daylight. When it came to resisting Victor's magnetic pull during a blackout, she was in deep caca. Hiding out in the bedroom wouldn't work. Mere feet away from a king-size paradise was the last place she needed to be. With the glow of the fireplace providing adequate lighting, she walked down the hallway and rejoined Victor in the main living space. She watched as he walked to the door and flicked the light switch. Nothing. He bypassed Maeve now in the hallway and went to the nightstand next to the bed. He pushed the button on the bottom of a lamp. Still no light. She retrieved her phone from where it had been charging in the bedroom.

"Yeah, we've lost power. My phone is no longer charging."

"It's probably only temporary," Victor offered. "Most hotels have backup generators.

"I hope so." She crossed over to a table, picked up the hotel phone and called the front desk. Moments later, the totally disheartened woman walked over to the blue flames that licked the glass enclosing it.

"The generator isn't working. A part they ordered months ago has yet to arrive."

"At least we've got the fireplace. Must be gas."

Victor looked over from where he'd walked to the window. "I can't believe the amount of snow that's fallen since we arrived. We could be snowed in for weeks, months."

"I doubt it's as bad as it looks," Maeve answered with a soft chuckle, joining him at the window. "This snow came down quickly. It is thick but powdery. That's a good thing. Unless it continues to fall at this rate or we experience a significant temperature drop, the road crews and utility companies should be able to respond to the covered roads and power issues fairly quickly."

Clearly, Maeve was no psychic. The weather report Victor found using his satellite phone contradicted everything she had assumed. The entire metropolitan area of Chicago was under a severe winter storm warning that included record-breaking snowfall for the next seventy-two hours along with temperatures set to drop below zero later that night. Citizens were warned against travel by car or foot. Pet owners were strongly encouraged to bring their furry friends inside. Even outside dogs were to be coaxed into garages. Because the snow would continue nonstop, it would be at least tomorrow morning before road crews began their work.

Maeve felt Victor's eyes on her. His gaze seared her skin and sent blood pumping into sensitive places.

"And if it doesn't?"

She swallowed and crossed her arms over nipples suddenly at attention. "I suggest we think positive and visualize being back in town."

"In the meantime…we've got tonight." Victor walked over to the table, where he removed the candles and a box of matches boasting the hotel's logo from the gift box. He lit the candles, then reached back into the gift box and pulled out the bottle of wine.

He nodded toward the kitchenette, then spoke to Maeve in a tone that brooked no argument. "There should be glasses in the cabinet."

"Who says I want wine?"

His gaze was searing, his eyes dark, challenging. "You don't?"

"Maybe a small glass. A drink. That's all I'm agreeing to. For everything else, this is an off-limits zone."

She whirled around and almost stomped to the kitchenette, but not before peeping the Cheshire cat smile on Victor's smug face. In that moment, she wished for dry roads, any other available room within walking distance—yes, in knee-deep snow—heck, even a room with double beds.

Actually, she longed for something even more unlikely, the willpower to resist Victor's irresistible charm. Even as she reached for the wineglasses, she knew that rejecting his inevitable advances was unlikely to happen. Because the only thing she wanted more than being able to resist him was to experience total surrender.

Eighteen

Victor managed to hide his smile. Maeve's mouth could say whatever it wanted but her eyes, attitude and body language told him all he need to know. She wanted him as much as he wanted her. And as much as she wanted to fight it, he knew how the night would end. The look in Maeve's eyes as she returned from the kitchenette suggested that she knew it, too. She placed the glasses on the table, then continued to the window.

"It's beautiful out here." Her voice was soft, silky, the way he imagined her skin beneath the bulky sweater. Suddenly, his hands itched to rub themselves against that skin, to reacquaint their touch with those unforgettable moments in Costa Rica now indelibly etched into his mind. He wasn't a schoolboy, though, so Victor kept his cool. He uncorked the bottle and filled their glasses, then walked to the couch in front of the fireplace. The perfect setting for seduction.

Victor prided himself on being a gentleman. A man of his word. He was disciplined, and had kept company with some of the world's most beautiful women. Yet at the moment, it took every ounce of strength that he possessed and some that he pulled from the ethers to follow Maeve's wishes and keep his hands off her. Did she have any idea how she looked in the firelight? How her mocha skin glowed in a way he wanted to lick it, and how her aroused nipples and desire-darkened eyes told him that her body hadn't agreed with anything she'd said? He looked over at the box Chef Kai had prepared and had had delivered and walked over just to distract himself.

He began lifting the lids off culinary snack masterpieces, from fresh lemon dill hummus to a white truffle/smoked, cheddar/maple bacon popcorn tin trio. "Well, at least we won't go hungry."

"Or cold," Maeve replied. She walked over to where housekeeping had placed extra blankets and a quilt.

"Just my luck that the generator isn't working."

"Or mine." At Maeve's chagrined expression, he chucked and added, "Just kidding."

Maeve stopped to look at him. "This isn't funny. My phone is less than fifty percent charged. Even with satellite, don't you think you might need your cell before we can get down the mountain?"

"Yes, but I'm not worried about access. It's self-charging."

"You have a self-charging cell phone?"

Victor had the humility to look a bit embarrassed. "A new technology that's been out for a while eliminates the need for chargers or batteries in most electronic devices."

"Why haven't I heard of it?"

"As you can imagine, there are companies out there not too thrilled at the prospect of being potentially put out of business."

Maeve nodded at the phone in his hand. "Is that it?"

Victor nodded.

"Mind if I check it out?" When he appeared to hesitate, Maeve added, "Don't worry. I'm not going to go into your text messages or emails and uncover the scores of naked women photos you've probably received."

"Well, in that case…" He handed her his phone.

Maeve made a big deal of examining it, turning it over in her hand. Victor played along, although the only energy in the room that had his attention was the sexual vibe flowing between them. To him, there was no way that she could not feel it, too. When she gave back his phone, he encircled her wrist.

"Come on. Let's sit down, enjoy our wine and the fireplace."

"I should probably keep my distance."

"Why? To try and prevent the inevitable from happening, and no, I'm not saying that because of my ego. It's because whatever differences that might exist between us, when it comes to intimacy, we're on the same page. I've never felt with any other woman the way I do with you. Us, together, is like magic. Tell me you feel differently."

Her voice came out in a whisper. "I can't."

He gently removed the phone from her hand and set it on the table, turned her around and began massaging her neck.

"You're tight."

"You think? Since arriving here, it's been one frustration after another."

He leaned forward, pushed her hair aside to kiss her neck, then placed his mouth close to her ear. "Let me help take care of that."

"Dammit, Victor." Maeve turned around, her look wary. "This is impossible."

"I know. But it's what we both want, and the perfect way to ward off the chill as the temperature drops."

"We're talking practicalities now?"

"An added benefit of lovemaking."

Maeve relaxed her shoulders, offered a brief smile. "One more time, that's it. What happens here, stays here. Once back in Chicago, I want your word that other than the case you will leave me alone."

"Okay."

"You promise?"

"I'll try."

"Victor…"

He kissed her lightly, inhaling her fragrance. "I'll do my

best to honor your wishes. That's the only type of promise I can keep."

Victor turned and began walking away.

"Where are you going?"

"Did you get a look at that tub? The hot water will work wonders on those tight muscles."

He felt no need to inform her about his strong, hard organ and how he'd soon be using it to remove any remaining kinks. Instead, he reached for their wineglasses and led them to the bedroom. He invited Maeve to relax while he got the bath ready. Once the tub began filling with steamy water, he poured in a liberal amount of bath salts and bubble bath from the gift box. Then he returned to the bedroom, undressed Maeve, slowly, deliberately, before picking her up, carrying her into the bath and placing her chilled naked body into a tub of bubbles. Maeve sighed, reached for a bath pillow and laid her head against the rim.

"Be right back." Victor retrieved the candles and after relighting them, placed them strategically around the tub. He quickly shed his clothes and joined her in the water. Reaching for a loofah, he rubbed it all over Maeve's body before using his hands to do the same. Later, in bed, there wasn't an inch of her that he didn't touch. He covered her chilled skin with a sheet, then scooted below it to dip his tongue into her heat. He sucked and licked and nibbled. She did the same, taking his sex into her mouth and driving him crazy. The sex was unhurried, thorough, satisfying. Outside, the snow continued to fall. In the bedroom, nothing but heat.

The next morning, with penis hard and body ready, Victor rolled over and reached for Maeve. Instead of the smooth flesh he imagined, his hand brushed cold rumpled sheets. Not exactly the wake-up he'd expected. He flopped on his back, expecting at any moment to hear the toilet flush and watch Maeve return to their love lair in all her naked glory. He stroked himself, smiling as he remembered how last night unfolded—how the outside temps dropped and the room got colder, and the ways they kept their bodies warm. Damn, he was ready for another round.

"Maeve!" He paused, listened, then sat up against the headboard. "Baby, where are you?"

Throwing back the covers, Victor climbed out of bed and sauntered naked into the living space. He was sure his bobbing member leading the charge would be enough to convince Maeve to stop whatever she was doing and rejoin him in bed.

Except… *Where is she?*

"Maeve?"

He walked into the bathroom. Remnants of Maeve having showered were there—opened toiletries on the counter, wet towels on the floor. Back in the living space, he walked its perimeter, though every inch of the luxurious area could be seen from the main room. It was several minutes before he noticed something he hadn't seen since last night. Lights. The electricity was back on. Only now he noticed Maeve's computer plugged in and turned on, along with the Keurig machine's blinking light. Now feeling like he was on a reconnaissance mission, Victor retrieved his jeans and sweater and dressed quickly. He returned to the bedroom where last night Maeve's phone had been charging. The charger station was empty. She had her phone. He picked his up from the nightstand beside the bed. He had just tapped her contact number when he heard the door open.

"Where have you been?" The combination of concern, exasperation and sexual frustration made the question come out harsher than he'd intended.

Maeve seemed undeterred, and even through the haze of sexual frustration, he realized she looked as bright as sunshine and fresh as a daisy. A band held a headful of bouncy curls away from her freshly scrubbed face. Her eyes were fairly sparkling and focused. She breezed by him on her way to the table as though he were barely in the room. And where had she gotten the new clothes?

He took a breath and joined her at the table, speaking again but this time with a calm voice. "I was worried about you."

"Sorry."

"Where were you?"

"Down at the business center."

"You were working?" She nodded. "On the case?"

"On this." She pulled a brief report from a folder and slid it across the table. "The facts to be presented to the judge next week."

"Why you want the case delayed."

"Why the case should be dismissed."

He looked up, got ready to speak, but considered the smug look on her face and decided it best to check out her findings. After reading the first paragraph, his stomach sank. Following the second one, he stood up and walked over to the window. The snow was still falling, covering last night's white blanket with a fresh coat, much as it appeared his client had covered up a major theft from his own grandmother. The thought didn't make Victor disappointed at potentially losing a case. It made him angry. He thought of his own grandmother and the close relationship they'd shared before she died. He thought of all the older women of his childhood, the village that helped raise him, especially after his parents separated.

He walked back to the table and sat down. "Hubert is connected to the Stone Mountain Trust."

"The second signer along with Daphne, his mother. My team is still trying to maneuver past the legal barriers to obtain more concise financial records, but there is a definite tie between that trust and a bank account Hubert set up in Las Vegas, which is connected to an offshore account. Of course, the identity of that account holder will never be uncovered, but we're fairly confident that a source we've recently located will help us put enough pieces of the puzzle together to make Hubert reconsider his lawsuit."

"Who's this source?"

Maeve sighed and for the first time since seeing her that morning, saw a dimming of the twinkle in her eye.

"His name is Louis Guitterez, a former employee who was obviously in cahoots with your client. He left rather abruptly a couple years ago and moved out of state. A PI located him just last night."

"And he admitted to taking part in a crime?"

"When initially questioned, I'm told he clammed right up. But the threat of federal charges of embezzlement, money laundering and the illegal transfer of funds, not to mention the possibility of a long prison sentence, worked to loosen his tongue."

"What exactly did he say?"

"He admits to working with Hubert while at the company and handling transactions that were questionable at best. He's agreed to being deposed without being subpoenaed but wants his own lawyer present."

"That's understandable."

"This storm will most likely prevent a personal meeting but we're hoping a virtual one can be set up as early as Tuesday."

Victor sat back, thoughtfully rubbing his chin. "This is crazy."

"Tell me about it. What a difference a day makes, huh?"

He reached for his phone. "Excuse me a moment."

"What are you getting ready to do?"

"Order room service. Then go to work. Looks like I need to set up a virtual conference of my own."

Victor ordered breakfast, then took a hot shower, still reeling from the turn of events. He should have been paying more attention to what her findings potentially meant for his client. But all he could think of was that once the case got dismissed, he and Maeve would no longer be opposing counsel. He'd be free to pursue her in a more serious manner and that's exactly what he intended to do.

Nineteen

Maeve couldn't believe the past twenty-four hours. How one moment she'd been arguing with Victor about winning the case, the next making mind-blowing love to the same man, and then, after seeing the blinking light on her cell-phone charger and realizing the electricity had come back on, picking up her phone and reading messages that immediately changed the trajectory of her day. Maybe her life. Her plans had changed from climbing back into bed with Victor for a leisurely sex-filled morning to coming out of the bathroom showered and dressed, her mind alert and fully in professional mode.

Shortly after contacting Raymond, Maeve carefully read the detailed report of his findings. She'd set up a conference call, then formulated a report outlining what Louis had told her. She'd gone downstairs to the hotel's small business center, where she'd printed out a formal copy of it for Victor and scheduled a second digital copy be sent via email to Judge Keller. Instead of requesting a delay, the email asked that the case be dismissed outright. Now, while waiting for all the players to gather and the video chat to start, Maeve half-heartedly munched on a croissant, looked around the room and finally allowed a brief recap of all that happened, and an honest assessment of how to proceed.

In the wee hours of the morning, while listening to the soft, satisfied slumber of her lover, Maeve had pondered her predicament. She was a woman in love (yeah, lust, too, but this feeling went way deeper than sex) with no idea of her next move. On one hand, the choice appeared simple. Date Victor secretly until the Duberry case was solved and a reasonable amount of time had gone by. Talk him into leaving his native Costa Rican paradise and join her in America. Ease him gently into Point du Sable society. Get her brothers to like him, so her currently distrusting family—and rightfully so—could get past his representation of a client against them. Lose her fear of giving over her heart. You know. Simple stuff. And then they could be together.

On the other hand, and there always had to be that other hand, the whole idea of a relationship with Victor was absurd. They lived on different continents. Maeve's roots in Point du Sable ran deep, as did Victor's in Costa Rica. Then there was that whole playboy lifestyle he'd admittedly led. Maeve's heart had already been shattered once in her life. She'd worked hard to get past Lionel and his betrayal, but deep down some of the fear invoked by her ex-fiancé's past actions still lingered. Victor was like fireworks. Fun, exciting, but what happened when the sparks died out? Did he move on and try to set someone else ablaze? Maeve didn't know whether the combustible possibility was worth the risk, or whether it would be better to choose someone like Matthias, a more predictable and steady flame.

"Good morning, sister."

Desmond's voice startled Maeve out of her reverie.

"Man, you were a million miles away. Already preparing for your next big case?"

"Something like that."

Desmond's comment had Maeve reaching for her cell phone. She tried for outward calm but inside her heart was racing.

"Hang on a minute, Des, I need to send this off to my assistant real quick."

She texted Victor.

Wherever you are, don't come back yet. On video conference. Family involved.

"Where are you?" Desmond asked.

"Stuck in the mountains. Mom didn't tell you?"

"Yeah, she told me. But I'm asking you."

"Still at the hotel. Snow is falling again, but it isn't as
heavy as yesterday. If it stops this afternoon as predicted,
the hotel believes the road crews will be able to do their
thing and allow us to come down the mountain tomorrow."

"Us?"

Crap! Maeve remained silent amid Desmond's narrow-
ing eyes.

"Mom said you went there for a meeting."

"That's right."

"Who with?"

"What's it to you?" Maeve jokingly asked, belatedly realizing she should have had a story ready.

"Because that's a long way to travel for a business meeting, that's why."

Jake entered behind Desmond and bopped his older
brother on the head. "Mind your business."

For his timing, Maeve could have kissed him.

"Now," Jake continued, sitting next to Desmond. "Who
in the hell did you sneak off with?"

"Unlike you, brother, every hotel visit isn't a booty call."

"Where's Victor?" Desmond asked.

"Good question," Maeve responded without missing a
beat. "Wherever that is, he'll be receiving a copy of the
motion to dismiss I'm preparing for Judge Keller."

"Desmond said you had good news. Who's the thief?"

"You didn't read the email I sent?"

"Why do that when I was coming on here?"

Raymond entered the call. He was in an office conference
room. The forensic accountant and two other team members
sat near him. "Good morning, everyone."

"You're in the office?" Maeve couldn't believe it.

"I'm a native Chicagoan," Raymond replied as though that explained everything.

"I'm a New Yorker," the forensic accountant, Sebastian, added.

"I'm trying for a promotion," noted the newest team member.

Everyone laughed and the meeting got underway. For the next forty-five minutes, Maeve was able to do what she hadn't done in twenty-four hours, not think about how Victor had claimed her—body and soul.

Victor sat in an unused office on the hotel's second floor, sipping coffee as he casually chatted with the twins, Adele and Agnes, waiting for their brother, Hubert III, to join the video call. He'd specifically chosen video over audio in order to see Hubert's physical reaction when he shared the news delivered by the Eddington Enterprise accountants and was thankful that for the sake of this conversation, the hotel's power had been restored.

"When was the last time you visited DC?" Adele asked, after sharing that Costa Rica was one of her favorite vacation destinations. She was the chattier of the two. Agnes was quiet, more cautious and reserved.

"Last year. I was invited by a friend to attend a party held at the Smithsonian's National Museum of African American History and Culture."

"Oh."

"Have you gone there?"

"Not yet."

"You should. It's a fascinating collection." He noticed the other twin engrossed on her cell phone. "What about you, Agnes?"

He asked not so much because he cared but to take his mind off Hubert's lateness to a meeting that should have held critical importance for the young man. Victor abhorred tardiness. Didn't like thieves much, either.

She looked up. "Huh?"

"Have you visited the Museum of African American History and Culture?"

"Yeah."

"What did you think?"

She shrugged. "It was cool."

Victor looked at his watch. "Did either of you speak with Hubert?"

"I just texted him again," Agnes responded.

"With last night's snowstorm, I know for a fact that he's definitely at home."

She reached for her phone. "Should I try calling him instead?"

A notification popped up on the computer screen. "No need. He just arrived. Let me allow him to enter…" Victor tapped a couple keys on the board. "Good morning, Hubert."

Hubert appeared to be still in bed. Again, Victor swallowed his anger. To control this meeting, he needed a calm head. Soon enough, he'd be rid of this spoiled client and never have to speak to him again.

"Glad you could join us," Victor said.

Hubert's response was a giant yawn as he rubbed his eyes. "It's early, man. Thought we were doing this next week."

"I apologize for the hour but the news I just received regarding your case necessitated this meeting."

"I hope that means you've exposed those crooks so I can get my money."

"Our money," Agnes emphasized.

Hubert leaned over and whispered something.

"Is someone with you?" Victor demanded.

"Yeah." Hubert's response dripped with defiance. "Why?"

"This is a private meeting, Hubert, regarding classified information. I need to share this information with you and your sisters, no one else."

"This is my girl," Hubert said, wrapping his arm around a woman whose face remained out of view. "She knows what's up."

"Either you find another room to participate in this meeting or I will continue with your sisters and email you a recap of what took place."

After a brief stare down, Hubert sighed. "Hold on a minute." His screen went black for several seconds. When it came back on, he was sitting on a couch.

"All right, tell us what this meeting is about. And get straight to the point. I've got things to do."

Victor ignored the insolence. His demeanor became serious as he leaned forward, toward the camera, and adopted a take-charge, superior posture.

"Hubert, Agnes, Adele, thank you all for joining me this morning for this impromptu meeting regarding recent developments pertinent to your case. As part of their investigation leading up to next week's hearing in the judge's chamber, the opposing counsel, Attorney Eddington and her team, hired a forensic accountant to conduct a thorough review of your grandmother's portfolio. That review has not been completed but he has uncovered something that might help move the case forward."

Victor steepled his hands, looked at Hubert and dropped the bomb-like information. "What is your relationship with Louis Guitterez?"

He watched as Hubert quickly covered a shocked reaction with a thoughtful frown. "Louis who?" he asked, rubbing his chin.

Victor had predicted Hubert would play the ignorance card. He tapped a key on his computer and shared the screen. A picture of Hubert and Louis appeared, standing in a club, sharing drinks and wide smiles.

"Oh, that dude. Um, yeah, we called him Luke. I know him. Not well, though. He spent some time in the Point.

Matter of fact, I think he did some work at Eddington Enterprise."

Settling into the story Victor imagined Hubert would be
sticking to, he relaxed against the sofa. "Our paths crossed
socially, a couple parties and whatnot." He pointed toward
the screen. "I think that pic was snapped at the Point Country Club."

"It was taken at CANN Casino in Las Vegas, Nevada,
two years ago in April, not long after Louis abruptly ended
his employment with Eddington Enterprise."

Second bomb, dropped. Target, hit.

Victor watched Hubert's face go from fair-skinned to
red to a dusky shade of gray. When finished, Hubert's
Adam's apple bobbed as he swallowed what Victor would
have guessed was a mouthful of fear.

"Oh, well, like I said, we socialized here and there. My
travel schedule is crazy. I hardly remember one country from
the next, let alone which city I visit in these United States."

Victor decided to give Hubert a chance to catch his
breath. He returned to speaker view, looked at the twins
and smiled. "Ladies, you're awfully quiet."

Adele, who he'd taken to privately calling Jada after
Maeve's reference to her and the famous actress looking
alike, shrugged her shoulders in a way to appear unbothered. "I don't have anything to add to that conversation."

"You never met Louis?"

She shook her head. "I don't ever remember meeting
him, which I would because he's kinda cute."

"I wish I could say his actions were equally attractive.
Agnes, what about you?"

Her glance toward her brother was so understated that
anyone less astute than Victor would have missed it.

"Maybe." Then sitting straighter in her chair, she added,
"I don't think so."

Victor once again shared the screen and revealed a ledger.
"These are transactions that over the course of several months

were transferred out of an account belonging to your grandmother and, through a series of moves, eventually ended up here."

Using a digital marker, he circled *Stone Mountain Trust*.

"Our grandparents lived in Georgia," Adele said.

Hubert exploded. "Did he ask us where they lived?"

Victor watched Adele frown, open her mouth to say something, then snap it closed. Agnes had retreated to her quiet space, a thumb sliding on the face of the cell phone she held.

"Agnes, Adele, I think for now that's all the questions I have for the two of you. Thanks again for making the meeting. I realize it's an hour earlier where you live."

"You're welcome, Victor," Adele said with a smile. "If you need anything else, let me know."

Agnes's goodbye was conveyed by leaving the meeting.

"Okay, Hubert, now that it's just the two of us, why don't you tell me what you know about Stone Mountain Trust."

"I don't know anything about it."

"That's interesting, especially since one of the accounts it's tied to is located in the same city where the picture of you and the ex–Eddington Enterprise employee's picture was taken. It also bears your name."

"I don't know what to tell you. The trust I'm attached to is the one Dad left for us. I don't know anything about one in Georgia."

"Fine, if that's the way you want to play it. But you should know that along with Eddington Enterprise, I will be handling my own investigation. I may not be able to crack into the offshore account in the Bahamas, the one that also has your fingerprints on it, but I will find out the truth. And when I do, it will go much easier for you if you're up front and honest with me now, instead of later. If the evidence convinces the judge to side in the company's favor, I wouldn't be at all surprised if you get hit with a lawsuit. Having them come after you would be bad enough. But having your former attorney testify on top of the evidence, could see you facing a federal indictment."

"I'm not worried about nothing," Hubert responded with feigned bravado.

He may have thought the nonchalant attitude the perfect smoke screen but the eyes didn't lie and Hubert's had fear stamped on each pupil. Victor ended the call, his thoughts divided as he gathered his things and prepared to leave the conference room. One set of thoughts were on the case facts as he now knew them. The others were on Maeve and what he wanted to do to her as soon as he returned to their suite.

Twenty

Maeve sat humming along with the tune coming from her tablet. It was an '80s hit that not only reminded her of her parents but also perfectly described her life right now. With the mounting evidence against Hubert, her company was almost sure to be exonerated and her family's reputation would remain intact. Finally, she'd come to a decision. She was going to let the past stay in the past. Without doing so, she'd have no future. Victor made her feel like none other. She'd be a fool to pass up the chance of a lifetime with someone like him because of the actions of another man.

Yes, sweet dreams were made of moments like this.

She looked up as the door lock disengaged. Victor came in smiling, looking like a man she could see come through a door every day for the rest of her life.

"Hey there."

"Hello, beautiful."

"I take it you've been working."

"Your take is correct."

"Telling your clients their game is over, I hope."

"Not so fast, Counselor. I'll need time to corroborate or refute what you're convinced is factual evidence."

Maeve sat back, twiddling a pen. "You're pretty sure, too. Otherwise, you wouldn't be so quick to investigate the information I sent over."

"What makes you think I am?"

"Your reputation as a top-rate attorney. Nobody gets your type of reputation without putting in the work."

"So you are aware of my stellar reputation."

Victor walked over with a look that suggested something other than court cases was on his mind. Maeve was all in.

"I've heard a thing or two," she purred, placing her hands in his to be lifted up.

"You can't believe everything you hear," he said, placing kisses on her face before sliding a tempting tongue along her cheek.

He pressed his crotch against her. "Can you believe this?"

"I declare," Maeve began, adopting a Southern drawl. "Is that the judge's gavel in your pants?"

Victor lifted Maeve off the floor. She wrapped her long legs around his waist, covering the lips he offered with her own. Last night, he was the aggressor. Now, Maeve swiped her tongue over his pillowy lips and then slid inside the opening. He cupped her ass. She groaned into his mouth, grinding her hips against him.

"I want you," she murmured with her lips still connected to his.

Victor walked them into the bedroom, placed her on the bed and began peeling off his shirt. Maeve reached for his belt buckle, her fingers shaking slightly as she worked to get it undone. Once that mission was accomplished, she pulled her top over her head and unsnapped her bra. Victor's slacks dropped to the floor. He stepped out of them. His sex bobbed and weaved as though impatient to be freed from its black boxer confines. Victor was just about to oblige said member when the phone rang.

Maeve reached for Victor's hand. "Don't get it," she panted.

Victor braced his hands on either side of Maeve's prone body, then slowly lowered himself down. "I didn't intend to."

The kiss was deep, possessive, perfect.

He cupped one of Maeve's breasts in his hand. His

thumb ran lazily over the nipple, causing it to harden and throb. Maeve ran her hand along Victor's back, down to his toned ass and back across his broad shoulders. Her body screamed to have Victor's hands roam it. She was hot for him, wet and hungry.

"I don't want to wait." He reached over to the nightstand and got one of several foil packets scattered on top it.

Maeve licked her lips. "Here, let me."

He shimmied out of his boxers.

Her phone rang.

Undeterred, Maeve kissed the tip of Victor's hardened shaft. She ran her fingers around the tip, looking at his rapidly changing expression as she positioned the condom over his dick and began rubbing him gently while sliding it down.

Victor's notifier went off.

"Hold on, baby." he stayed her hand. "I need to check out whose calling."

"Why?"

Maeve reached for him, but Victor slid out of bed. He retrieved his phone from the other room. A few seconds later, she heard him talking.

"Hey, man, what's up?"

He walked back into the room and mouthed, *Cornelius.*

Maeve's eyes widened slightly. She rolled out of bed, pulling on her top as she went to check out the call she'd missed.

"What you're asking is confidential information, Cornelius. I can't get into that."

Maeve went back to the bedroom and put a finger over her mouth. She showed him the missed call.

Cornelius.

He pressed the speaker button on his phone. "Hubert isn't satisfied with your representation. Says that Maeve is going to push to have his lawsuit thrown out and that you didn't seem to have a strategy to combat that move."

"I'm handling the case as I see fit, based on the facts as I understand them right now."

"He doesn't think you like him. He thinks that's why you're so keen on having the case dismissed."

"That's not true."

"Even so, he doesn't trust you. Feels you might sabotage his case."

"Do you want it? Because if so, I'll be more than happy to turn it over. Have Hubert call me with that directive or even better, email it so that I have it in writing, and I'll forward the case files tonight."

"Sounds like Hubert's right. You don't want to work on his behalf."

"Don't make this my decision. He's the one who seems to suddenly want another attorney. I'm only trying to please my client by giving him exactly what he desires. Maybe it would be better if you took it over. If not dismissed, the case will at least be delayed. I can have the physical files on your desk as soon as I'm back on Monday."

Both Maeve and Victor flinched at his snafu.

"Back? Where are you?"

"Hey, I had to get out of Chicago." Victor's answer was as glib as it was noncommittal. "You know I can't take the snow."

"I've also tried reaching Maeve, both last night and this morning. Do you know where she is?"

"As a matter of fact, I think I do."

Maeve swatted Victor's arm. He bit back a laugh.

"Where? Wait, are the two of you together?"

"I didn't say that, brother. I said I think I know where she is."

Liar, Maeve mouthed, then kissed his cheek.

"When she sent over the information that led to the conference call that has Hubert upset, she mentioned being stuck at a hotel because of the snow."

"Chicago got hit pretty bad," Cornelius mumbled. Maeve could imagine the flurry of thoughts running through her friend's astute mind.

"Bad enough for the place to lose power. She said they just got back internet this morning."

"I did hear about power outages last night on the news. But the Chicago hotels I know about all have generators."

"I'm not familiar enough with the situation to know one way or the other."

Maeve wrapped herself around Victor. She began sliding a hand down his rock-hard torso to something becoming equally hard a few inches below the would-be belt. Victor reached over and tweaked one of the hardening nipples protruding from her top.

"Do you want it or not?"

"What?"

"The case. I don't want to work for a client who doesn't believe I have his best interest at heart."

"Do you?"

"I'll admit that I think Hubert's a spoiled brat who needs a good dose of tough love to help him grow up. But on top of being an honest lawyer, something that is considered almost an oxymoron, I'm also a man of integrity. I always work from the angle of doing what's best for my client. In this instance, having the charges dropped and the case dismissed may be in Hubert's and his sisters' best interest."

Maeve was ready to end this conversation. She pushed Victor onto his back, removed the condom and began licking his lollipop.

"Look, man, I gotta go."

Maeve pulled his tip into her mouth, then began sliding down the length of his engorged shaft.

"Why don't we set up a meeting for Monday at the club."

"Ah! That's cool."

"What time?"

"Whatever works for you," Victor eked out in a rush.

Maeve fondled his sac, ran a fingernail across his inner thigh.

"I need to take this other call."

Victor ended the conversation without saying goodbye. With a single motion, he flipped them over with Maeve on her back, re-sheathed himself and plunged in to the hilt. He was still for several seconds as Maeve's tight body pulsed and relaxed around his size. She felt herself open up and lifted her hips to encourage his continuation.

"Now, where were we," she whispered, the words hot and wet in his ears.

"Right here," he said, adopting a slow, steady rhythm with deep soul-stirring thrusts. "Exactly where we're supposed to be."

Maeve raised her legs so that Victor could go deeper. There was a lot to work out if they decided to get serious but in this very moment, with him making love to her so fully and completely, she couldn't agree with him more.

The next morning, having worked up quite the appetite, Victor ordered in breakfast. He went back in the room, intent on yet another round of lovemaking. Would he ever tire of her? He shook her shoulder slightly. Maeve moaned and turned over. She looked so beautiful, so peaceful in sleep, that he didn't have the heart to wake her. Instead, he took a long hot shower. When breakfast arrived, he tipped the employee, rolled the cart into the bedroom and, after retrieving a hot washcloth from the bathroom, shook Maeve again.

"Wake up, sleepyhead."

Her eyes slowly batted open, a move Victor decided he could see every morning for the next fifty or so years.

"Here, wash your face."

Maeve sat up, reached for the towel with a yawn. "What time is it?"

"A little after ten?"

"What?"

Victor laughed. "I make no apologies for wearing you out last night. But your body needed the rest."

"And I need a bathroom."

She stood and looked over his shoulder. "What's that?"

"Breakfast. Hurry up."

Maeve returned to the room wearing a towel, with water trickling down from her still-damp hair. Victor had pulled up the spread, turning their love lair into an equally private picnic.

Maeve sat across from him. "I'm starved."

She picked up one of several silver domes. The aroma of a veggie and sausage quiche filled the air. For the next several minutes, they concentrated on food—filling plates and satisfying appetites. Once finished, Victor moved everything back to the tray and pulled Maeve into his arms. He inhaled the jasmine in the shampoo she'd used on her hair and forced his body not to react.

"You know you did this on purpose."

Maeve's head jerked up. "Did what?"

"Brought me here. Didn't you say you were born and raised in Illinois?"

"Yes. And?"

"You knew what kind of storm we were in for, were certain that once up the mountain we wouldn't be able to get down it. You planned to take advantage of me all along and just needed a reason to justify it in your own mind."

"You are so off base."

"I'm reading your cards and you know it. But it's all good, though. I'll be your captive anytime."

"All right, captive. Shut up and kiss me."

For once, the lip-lock exchange didn't lead to making

love. Instead, the two got dressed, made mugs of steaming hot cocoa and sat in front of the fireplace to get to know each other more.

"When's your birthday?" Maeve asked.

"October ninth. Yours?"

"February twenty-second."

"Right around the corner." Maeve nodded. "I should throw you a party."

"You'd do that?"

"Yeah, as long as you and I are the only guests." Maeve gave him a look. "Hey, I can't help it if I want to keep you all to myself. Will you come back to Costa Rica to celebrate?"

"I'd love to."

"So how old will you be, forty?"

He dodged a punch.

"Twenty-nine, thank you very much. So you've got that forty-something lane all to yourself."

"Ha! Not quite, darling. I just turned thirty-four."

"How many serious relationships have you had?"

"Define *serious*."

"Mutually exclusive. Long-term. Engagements. That sort of thing."

"None really."

"You're kidding."

Victor sipped his chocolate while running through his index of romantic entanglements. "There's one girl I dated off and on for years. She got married a few years back, then divorced. We started seeing each other again, but only casually. I don't think I'm the marrying kind."

"That's too bad."

"Why, you want to marry me?"

"No."

He reached for her. "You're just going to use my body for mind-blowing sex and then throw me to the wolves?"

Maeve nestled against him. "Something like that."

Victor wrapped his arms around her as a comfortable silence descended. A Bill Withers tune popped into his head, causing him to smile. Indeed, if getting used felt this good, Maeve Eddington could use him up. He wouldn't complain to anybody. At all.

Twenty-One

It was late Monday evening when Maeve got into her car and headed down the mountain. Being extra cautious, especially after the conversation with Cornelius, Victor decided to order a car service so the two of them could arrive back in town separately. Neither put the possibility of prying eyes being everywhere out of their minds. They were too close to being able to date openly to take any chances. A week from now, two weeks max, the case should wrap up and Maeve and Victor could go on with their lives. Together. She'd celebrate her birthday in his country. Maeve hadn't been this excited about a relationship since…in a very long time. She couldn't wait to share her happiness. As soon as she left behind the two-lane road and reached the interstate, she began returning a slew of missed phone calls, beginning with Reign.

"About time you called!" was Reign's hello. "Didn't you get any of my messages or texts saying I had something very important to tell you?"

"Yeah, well, I have something important to tell you, too. Besides, Mom knew I'd gotten snowed in. I'm sure she told you guys."

"I knew about that. Saw the news and knew that power went out, too. But that was Friday night. Mom said power was back on the next day."

"I'm sorry for not calling back. There's a lot going on."

"Jake told me about Hubert stealing the money, and that the case would be dismissed."

"It's not all wrapped up and tied with a pretty bow just yet but all indicators point in Hubert's direction as the culprit, enough to at least get us off the hook. But that's not the biggest news from the weekend."

"No, I've probably got that."

"I doubt it." Maeve couldn't stop the smile that broke out on her face. "I'm in love."

The briefest of pauses and then, "Maeve, you need to know that—"

"Didn't you hear what I just said, Ms. Celebrate in Every Position? The one who encouraged me to let go of the past and trust love again? Well, I did and I am, sis, and let me tell you, it's amazing."

"I'm really happy for you, Maeve."

"You don't sound like it."

"It's just that—"

"That what? I didn't call you sooner or respond to your texts?" Maeve continued in a rush of euphoria. The more excited she became, the faster she talked.

"I wanted to, believe me there were so many times over the weekend that I thought about what you'd said. I know it's the big sisters who usually get credit for helping the younger ones but this time our roles were reversed. You helped me push past my fear and really open my heart. Now it's bursting with joy. I can't remember ever being this happy. Victor is amazing, sister. And not just the physical part but emotionally, intellectually—"

"Lionel's here."

"You wouldn't think a guy like him has a sense of humor but…"

As though in slow motion, what Reign last spoke finally caught up with Maeve's hearing. "What did you say?"

"Lionel. He's returned home, divorced and determined to win you back."

"What?"

"That's why I blew up your phone with back-to-back calls! He came over Friday, unannounced, just as the storm hit. Talked with Mom and Dad for hours. Ended up spending the night."

"Shut. Up."

"We spent most of Saturday in the game room, him spilling his heart out all over Mom's prized Persian rug, apologizing over and over, especially to Desmond, who treated him like a brother, and saying what a mistake he'd made."

"And they accepted it?"

"Not really. They grilled him pretty hard but all he'd say was that there was more to the story than we knew years ago and that you deserved to be the first one who heard it. He's convinced that once you do, all will be forgiven and you two will ride off into the sunset. He begged for your number. We didn't provide it, of course."

"Maeve, you there?"

"I can't believe this. Just when I finally feel like I'm over his ass. Why'd he have to come back now?"

"I agree. The timing sucks."

As the news continued to sink in, Maeve's shock turned to anger. "If he thinks he can waltz back into my life and take up where we left off, he has another think coming. I'm not sure I even want to see him, much less hear the pathetic explanation he's had five years to create on why he broke off our engagement with a text."

"My sentiments exactly."

"And the nerve of him to show up at the Estate uninvited! Mom and Dad should have turned him away, forced him to make an appointment."

"As close as they are to his parents? They'd never do that."

"I know."

Images from the past rushed into Maeve's mind. How at one time she and Lionel practically lived at each other's houses. How much she'd loved his parents. How easily Lionel had fit into the Eddington clan. College and the challenge of a long-distance relationship, the planning of their wedding part of the glue that held them together. Graduating, returning to Point du Sable and home-shopping. The Fourth of July weekend that changed everything.

Maeve's call-waiting indicator pinged. She looked at the dash.

Victor. Just. Great. There was no way Maeve could talk to him while on such an emotional roller-coaster ride.

"I'm getting a headache."

"Sorry to ruin your great weekend."

"Not your fault. I'm almost home. Let's talk then."

Back in Point du Sable, Maeve talked and talked and talked. With Reign. With Derrick and Mona. With Desmond and Jake. Separately and together, they mulled over the unexpected reappearance of Dr. Lionel B. Young, Maeve's high school and college sweetheart, first lover and ex-fiancé. Finally, drained and with a tremendous workload for the week ahead, Maeve shut down the topic and for the second time that weekend forced her mind away from a man to concentrate on the case. Law had not only long been Maeve's passion but now, as when Lionel jilted her, work was her saving grace. An email to the judge requesting a dismissal of the lawsuit had been sent over earlier that morning. Maeve completed the paperwork for the official filing, which she'd present to the court clerk tomorrow morning. She opened her office email account, forwarded some to her assistant to handle, including setting up a lunch meeting with a potentially lucrative corporate account, and answered others from colleagues or longtime customers. Finally, she sent Victor a text.

Hey handsome. Saw you called. Sorry, couldn't return it. Crazy busy. It's back home and back to business so...see you in court. :)

Maeve read it a second time, and then a third. Convinced that it held the right balance of flirtation and seriousness, the complete opposite of how she really felt, she pressed Send and hoped that he wouldn't try to call her again tonight. She hoped a good night's sleep would help her gain a better perspective of how to juggle a past love with her potential future happiness.

It didn't, so the following morning Maeve did the next best thing—a Mona move. She dressed for success. The funkiness of the wide-legged winter white suede pantsuit she chose was toned down with a navy shell, low-heeled navy ankle boots, a single strand of multi-colored Tahitian pearls and her straightened hair pulled back into a ponytail tightly secured at the nape. She slid on a favorite navy mohair coat, threw a printed raw silk scarf around her shoulders and on the way to the courthouse listened to a self-affirming, life-invigorating anthem for women, the latest by Jan Baker, a neo-soul standout. She arrived at the classically inspired Point du Sable Courthouse in the center of the town square feeling unsure of her personal life but in control of what was getting ready to take place in the judge's chambers.

Maeve parked her car and hurried inside. The day was overcast, the temperature, freezing. The heels of her cute boots *click-clacked* across the black-and-white tile. She stopped at the security station, greeted the officer, removed her coat and placed her purse and briefcase on the short conveyor belt. On the other side, she gathered her things and quickly proceeded down the hall to the judge's chamber. After a light tap on the door, she opened it and went inside. As chambers went, Judge Keller's was quite spacy. Yet, as soon as she looked up, all she saw was Victor. His presence took up the entire room. It was hard to think, to breathe. The certainty gained during their snowbound tryst was shattered. The feeling she'd had coming down the mountain, that life was sweet and perfect and that she knew exactly how to proceed, no longer there.

Lionel's back.

Those two words had changed everything. Brought back all the emotions she'd experienced with him in the almost seven years they'd spent together, even longer if you counted their childhood. That fact had helped Maeve realize why it was so hard to shake him. She'd known and loved Lionel practically her entire life.

She wasn't aware she'd stopped just inside the door until Victor began walking toward her. He opened his arms for an embrace. She sidestepped him.

"Hello, Victor."

A pause and then, "Good morning, Counselor."

Because she'd continued farther into the space, Maeve missed the look of hurt and confusion that flashed in Victor's eyes. Again, he walked to her, close enough to speak softly. He placed a gentle hand on her arm so that she couldn't walk away.

"After our last…meeting… I thought a mere handshake inappropriate."

"We're opposing counsel. One could say it would be inappropriate for us to touch at all." With that, she took a step back, tried to gain her equilibrium in her personal space.

"The judge is late?"

Victor eyed his watch. "We've got a couple minutes."

"This shouldn't take long."

Maeve began to remove her coat. She felt rather than saw Victor come behind to assist. Her body stiffened of its own accord. She hoped he didn't notice.

He did.

"Are you okay?"

"I'm fine," she lied, reaching for the coat he now held and placing it on a nearby coat-tree before sitting down.

If Victor's expression was any indication, he didn't believe her for one minute. Maeve felt that if she could keep the meeting in professional and not personal waters, they could get through it okay.

"Have you spoken further with your clients?"

Victor eyed her a beat longer before going along with her obvious attempt to redirect the conversation.

"They know about today's official filing of the motion to dismiss. Hubert isn't happy with my decision. Wanted to replace me with Cornelius, as you know. Did you ever return his call?"

Maeve shook her head. "I texted him, explained my busy schedule and underscored what you'd shared about the case. He seemed okay with it."

"If you ask me, I think his feelings for you run deeper than friendship."

"Who asked you?" A smile reduced the sting of her words and thawed the atmosphere. Perfect timing as the judge entered amid those smiles.

"Good morning Attorneys Cortez, Eddington." Judge Keller, a black robe thrown over a sweater and jeans, took her seat behind a massive oak desk. "I understand that we're here today to entertain a motion to dismiss?"

"That is correct, Judge." Maeve handed the judge a folder. "Here is the physical copy of that which was mentioned over the weekend and emailed this morning."

The judge took a quick moment to scan the document.

"Any argument?" she asked Victor.

"Not at this time, however, I'd ask that the case be dismissed without prejudice in the event additional information that could change this week's decision be brought to light."

"At this time, you both agree that one or more of the plaintiffs were involved in absconding with the money outlined in the lawsuit, that one of the heirs, and not anyone from Eddington Enterprise, is responsible for its disappearance?"

"That is correct, Your Honor," Maeve said.

"Yes, Judge," Victor agreed.

The judge looked at Maeve. "Given this strong probability, will there be any countersuits such as defamation or criminal charges filed on behalf of Eddington Enterprise?"

"The exact steps to be taken once the case has been dismissed have not yet been discussed. Because the case seems to have been kept under wraps, we've not experienced public slander or damage to the company's professional reputation. I would like a meeting to be scheduled with the claimants so that the details of this matter remain private, possibly through an NDA or gag order from the court."

"Any objection to that?" Judge Keller asked Victor.

"I'd like to be present at that meeting."

"Of course."

"I'll review the materials you've provided and make a decision this week. Is there anything else?"

Maeve felt Victor's eyes on her. She looked straight ahead. "That's all for me, Judge Keller."

"Nothing for me at this time. Oh, one thing. With this case being finalized, at least for now, I will most likely be returning to Costa Rica. I'd like to request that sufficient notice be given for any subsequent meetings taking place here in Illinois."

"That's reasonable, Counselor. There is also the option of attending the meeting via video conference, although—" the Judge fixed Victor with a look that Maeve thought less than professional "—we'd much rather see you in person."

"I appreciate that, Judge," Victor replied in that silky voice that brought moisture to women's lady parts. Maeve could have smacked him. And the judge.

"Then court is adjourned." The judge banged her gavel and rose from the chair. "Be careful out there you two. I hear another storm is on the way."

Looking at Victor, Maeve couldn't have said it better. In fact, the storm was already here.

Twenty-Two

The minute Maeve entered the chambers, Victor knew something was different. He also would have bet his law license that whatever it was had nothing to do with the case. It was as though he could fairly feel the tension in her body, even before he provided assistance in removing her coat. The body he knew could be pliable and limber had felt as stiff as a board. Now with the judge gone and the two of them alone, the tension and discomfort had returned.

"What's going on, Maeve?"

"A hearing to have a lawsuit dismissed that should never have been filed. Actually, I think it went quite well."

Victor frowned. Was she back to giving attitude as though he were the opposing attorney and nothing more? After their holiday rendezvous and the weekend they'd shared? Victor wondered what was really going on.

"I mean with you personally. Something is different. I felt it as soon as you walked in the door."

"Who are you? Miss Cleo's cousin? You know, mon, from Jamaica?" She added an exaggerated accent imitating the TV psychic that made Victor laugh out loud.

"Woman, a deaf and blind man would have known that someone highly upset had entered the building. But you don't want to talk about it."

"Yes, something is going on and no, I don't want to talk about it. Not here. Not now."

"What about over breakfast?"

"Can't. Back-to-back meetings."

Maeve reached for her coat. Victor reached to take it away from her. Their fingers touched. The moment sizzled. He slid the coat up her arms and gave her body a light squeeze before stepping away.

"What about lunch?"

"Another meeting. I wasn't exaggerating when I left you the crazy busy text. When I finally went through my work in-box last evening, it was filled with stuff to do."

"Dinner, then."

When it came to the opposite sex, Victor had never had to work for much of anything, especially a date. Under normal circumstances, he would have said his goodbyes and pulled out the little black book that over the past few months had gotten too little use. But nothing about him and Maeve was normal. No other woman had made him feel the way she did. No one else had made him want to be a problem-solver, dream-maker, the proverbial knight in shining armor he'd been convinced had not existed. He wanted to be one now.

Maeve began walking. He fell into step beside her. "Did you park in the garage or on the street?"

"I snagged a space right in front of the building."

"I'm in the garage. Come with me and I'll drive you to your car."

"How gallant of you but really, Victor, I think I can handle the distance between the front door and my vehicle."

"You might be able to, but I can't." He grabbed her hand, bypassed the elevator and headed for the stairs.

"Let me go," she hissed under her breath.

"Don't make a scene," he replied, his face one of pleasant calm as he nodded at a deliveryman.

Maeve cooperated down the flight of stairs but once in the garage, removed her hand from his grasp.

"I told you, I've got meetings."

"This won't take long."

They reached his rental. He tapped the fob and opened the passenger door. Maeve reluctantly got in. Victor quickly rounded the car and entered on the driver's side. He started the car and began talking as it warmed.

"Talk to me, Maeve. Something is going on with us. After sharing our hearts with each other this weekend, I think I deserve to know what it is."

Maeve took a deep breath, looked straight ahead.

"Baby, please."

He watched her face and its changing expressions. Finally, she looked down at her hands and said, "My ex is back."

The words hit like a punch in a gut. Victor would have preferred the physical version. Yet, he tried to keep his voice light, casual. Clearly, Maeve was already suffering enough.

"Ex-boyfriend?"

"Fiancé."

"I didn't know you were engaged to be married."

"We hadn't made it official, thankfully. Only the people in our inner circles knew he'd proposed."

"What happened?"

Maeve shrugged. "I don't know."

"What did he say when you asked him?"

"Back then I never got the chance."

"And now that he's returned? I assume you two have talked."

She looked over and gave a quick shake of her head. Her expression made everything in him want to confront the person who'd dared hurt her like this, and to love all that hurt away.

"I don't know that it's a question that needs to be answered. What does it matter?"

Maeve looked out the window, and Victor slipped into vivid memories of yesterday.

"At the end of the day, that's the truth of it. I thought

we were happy, solid. We'd dated since high school and had been good friends before that. He and Desmond played sports together. His family and mine are friends. Then one day…"

Her voice trailed off. Victor patiently waited. She'd speak when she was ready. For her, right now, he had all the time in the world.

"He went out of town, to Washington, DC. A family obligation he told me, a favor for one of his dad's fraternity brothers and longtime family friend. The friend had daughters. One got pregnant. He had left me and married her before I knew any of this. They settled in another state. I went on with my life."

"You should continue going on with it." He reached over and placed a hand over hers. "With me, and what began in earnest this past weekend."

Maeve slowly turned her hand so that they could clasp fingers. She showed the first true smile he'd seen all day. "I think you're right."

Victor felt the urge to crow like a rooster. "You do?"

She nodded. "What's past is past. I want to focus on the present."

Pausing, she outlined the strong veins that ran along the top of his equally strong hands. "Honestly, I don't know about the future. But when it comes to my life right now, I see you in it."

Those words caused a burst of something indefinable in his heart yet quite recognizable in his loins. He couldn't wait another second to touch her. He leaned over and was pleased when she met him halfway. Their kiss was gentle, loving, filled with promise. It felt like a symbolic seal on that promise and made him feel less angst about returning to Costa Rica because he knew that in a little more than a month she'd join him there. Coming from a family like hers, he was sure Maeve had experienced some amazing birthday celebrations. But he planned to do everything in his power to make sure none would ever top the first one she experienced with him.

Maeve looked at her watch. "We really should go."

Victor started the car. "What about dinner tonight?"

"Is it okay to call you later? I'll have a better idea of my schedule after lunch."

"I guess I can wait that long."

He pulled out of the underground parking garage into a day that threatened more snowfall.

"As much as I love being wherever you are, I can't wait to get back to sunshine."

"I don't blame you. Chicago winters are definitely no joke."

"Did your family suspect anything about your being stuck in the mountains?"

"Of course," she said with a laugh that Victor could record, put on loop and play him out of a deep depression. "Mom wasn't too curious, or at least it didn't show. Desmond wondered what client I'd be meeting in such an isolated place."

"What about your sister?"

"She knows about us."

"Ah, so you tell me to keep this under wraps while you're busy letting the cat out of the bag."

"She most deserves to know the truth. It was her nagging at me to get on with my life that opened me up to dating you."

"Dating? Is that what we're doing?"

"I don't know what we're doing, but I like it."

For Victor her words were like sunshine piercing the clouds.

"My car's right there."

"Out of the sedan and back into the sporty number. It suits you."

"Are you saying I seem to like the fast lane?"

"I'm saying that, like you, it has nice curves, though

your body is sleeker and sexier than any automaker could ever design."

"I never thought someone complimenting me would include a car description but thanks, I think."

Victor laughed as he leaned over for another kiss. Maeve hurriedly opened the door and got out."

He rolled down the passenger window. "So I can't be kissed in broad daylight?"

"Not until the case is officially over." She leaned into the window and lowered her voice. "After that we can make love in the middle of the square."

"I'm going to hold you to that," he yelled at her retreating frame.

Victor watched until Maeve got into her car, started it up and gave a little wave. He headed down Main Street, then feeling the need to release pent-up energy, pulled over and tapped his phone.

"Cornelius, good morning. What are you doing?"

"Having breakfast. What about you?"

"Just left the courthouse. The motion to dismiss has been filed. I called to see if you were up for a game."

"I will be in a couple hours."

"Cool. See you then."

Victor headed away from the direction of the interstate on-ramp and drove through the clean picturesque streets of Point du Sable on his way to the country club where he and Cornelius would play tennis. Passing the high school, he imagined Maeve growing up in a town that screamed wealth and security, where one could imagine their dreams coming true. He took in the upscale architecture and immaculate streets where there wasn't a fast-food joint in sight. While stopped at a traffic light, he noticed a restaurant in one of the contemporarily designed buildings and on a whim decided to eat there instead of the country club dining room. He put on his signal, slid into the right-hand lane and turned into the establishment's parking lot.

"Good morning! Table for one?" asked the perky young woman sporting turquoise hair when he stepped up to the hostess stand.

Victor nodded toward the counter. "One of those stools is fine."

She handed him a menu. "Take your pick."

"Thank you."

After a quick scan of a menu filled with all organic keto, paleo and vegetarian choices, he placed his order then pulled out his phone and began checking emails. He was in the middle of responding to one when his peaceful, perfect morning was interrupted.

"Well, good morning there, handsome! I guess today is my lucky day!"

Not again. Victor looked up. "Camela. Are you stalking me?" His smile belied how much he believed the question held real possibility.

"No, but I should. Since you haven't returned any of my calls, it seems the only way we can talk. A friend of mine who lives here just had a baby. I came to see her. Much better seeing you."

He allowed the hug she was determined to give him, and hoped he wouldn't asphyxiate from the perfume she'd obviously bathed in.

"Is anyone sitting here?" she asked, sliding onto the bar stool beside him.

"If they are, you're now sitting on their lap" was his wry reply.

"I'd much rather sit on yours."

If Victor hadn't already ordered, now is when he'd have made his exit. But he'd dealt with women much deadlier than Camela. She represented the exact type of energy he didn't want in his life. Dinner and hopefully a nightlong dessert with Maeve later would more than make up for the hour of chitchat he was forced to deal with now. If he played his cards right, he'd spend a lifetime with his favorite attorney while the woman now blabbing beside him would soon be nothing more than an unpleasant memory.

Twenty-Three

After a quick meeting with her assistant and another with Raymond and the team, Maeve left the offices for her lunch meeting at the Point Country Club. She hummed a love song as she walked to her car and once on the short drive to her destination, couldn't stop smiling. Being with Victor did that to her. So did making a decision that felt right to her heart without allowing her head to talk her out of it. Last night, the shock of hearing that Lionel had returned to Point du Sable had threatened to unravel the newfound, tenuous romance she'd found with Victor. Memories of her first true love and how their relationship ended had stirred up all the emotions, insecurities and doubt that had kept Maeve mostly single for the past three years. Victor not only reminded her of the love she'd missed out on but had also opened the door to a feeling she'd never experienced. Being with him made Maeve realize that while she had fiercely loved Lionel, she may not have been in love with him. If she had been, then what was this overwhelming, all-consuming feeling she had for Victor? She didn't know, but Maeve would happily agree to spending a lifetime finding out, starting with tonight. She texted him her address and told him dinner would be served at her house…in her bed.

Reaching the valet stand at the Point Country Club, Maeve all but skipped into the dining facility. Her client had reserved one of the small private rooms for today's meetings, a common occurrence among those not wanting the town all up in their business. Especially companies with rivals who often dined at the same place. Maeve was aware of several firms who absolutely abhorred each other but put their trust along with their money into the financial services of Eddington Enterprise.

"Good afternoon, Ms. Eddington," the hostess said. "You look bright and cheery today."

"I'm feeling bright and cheery, despite the weather."

"It's looking downright gloomy outside. Another snowstorm may be on the way."

"That's what I heard. I'm here for a twelve o'clock meeting with—"

"Mr. Bruce Parker. He arrived a short while ago and is waiting in the Nine Iron room. I can take you there if you'd like."

"That's quite all right." Maeve was well acquainted with the hallway of private rooms boasting golf-term names.

"Asking is a requirement, Ms. Eddington. I see you here all the time and know you can find your way around."

"Enjoy your day," Maeve said, the smile she'd given the hostess still on her face as she made her way down the hall. Passing the Fairway room, Maeve's mind went back to her last time there and her shock at seeing Victor at the meeting of lawyers. On that day, she'd had no idea how that meeting would change her, lead her to another professional victory and into the arms of the man who could very well become the love of her life. She reached the Nine Iron room and with a hand on the door handle, took a second to wipe what felt like a goofy smile off her face. Time to adopt a professional air. She opened the door and saw a man with his back to her, gazing out the window. Something about him gave her pause, caused her heart to seize up slightly in her chest. As quickly as the feeling happened, she berated herself for imagining things and stepped deeper into the room. The man turned around.

Lionel.

"Hello, Maeve."

On instinct, Maeve turned back toward the door she'd just entered. Hurried footsteps were followed by a hand on her arm.

"Maeve, wait."

She jerked her arm out of his grasp. "How dare you trick me into a meeting with you."

"Please forgive me," he quickly replied.

Maeve saw a swirl of emotions in his eyes, sincerity being one of them. She took a deep breath and forced herself to relax.

"I—I didn't think you'd come otherwise."

"You're right."

"There's so much I want to say to you, Maeve. That I need to tell you."

"Don't you think it's a little late for that?"

"I'd like to believe it's never too late."

He reached for her hand. Maeve sidestepped him and walked to a framed picture that dominated the wall. A thousand thoughts raced through her mind. She couldn't capture a single one of them.

"I'm sorry, Maeve. You'll never know how sorry I am. If I said those words a million times, it wouldn't be enough."

She whirled around. "Then why even try? Why put us through the pain of dredging up a past we can't change? Because your marriage is over you suddenly have room for me? You think you can come back into my life and pick up where you left off, now that the woman you left me for has left you?"

"I divorced her, Maeve."

"Oh, well, that makes all the difference. I don't give a damn what happened in your marriage, or that it didn't work out. It doesn't change what happened to us, how you dumped me, via text message no less, and never looked back."

"Maeve, I—"

"Not a phone call, or an email, not even another text to lessen the pain of the one that delivered the kill shot."

"I never stopped thinking of you, caring about you, asking after you. I spoke to your brother Desmond—"

Maeve snorted.

"He was incredibly upset with me, as you can imagine."

"Oh, I was there. I don't have to imagine it."

"He told me in no uncertain terms to leave you alone, that I had hurt you enough."

"And you listened? You'd broken up with the girl who gave you her virginity, who invested in you with almost half of her life and her brother's feelings were the ones that caused you concern?"

"He threatened me, Maeve. Said you didn't want anything to do with me. Why would you? I believed him. After the way that I hurt you, it was easy to imagine you not wanting to talk to or see me again."

"I deserved more."

"You did. You do."

The door opened with a server pushing a tray. He stopped as though barred on entering farther by the tension in the room.

"Should I come back later?" he asked.

Lionel held up a hand to the server, his eyes on Maeve. "Please, Maeve, can we sit down?"

Maeve huffed, took pity on the obviously uncomfortable server and walked to the table. Out of the corner of her eye, she saw Lionel's subtle signal to the waiter, who gave Maeve a tenuous smile as he neared the table.

She returned it. "Charlie, right?"

His eyes widened slightly. "Why yes, Ms. Eddington. I didn't think you'd remember."

"How could I forget the level of service you gave us during my sister-in-law's birthday dinner. Ivy still talks about your sweet serenade."

Charlie's face reddened at the praise. Lionel quietly took a seat on the other side of the table. Maeve ignored him.

"You're still pursuing your music, right?"

Charlie nodded. Maeve could see his shoulders relax as he poured out two glasses of lemon water and set a basket of rolls on the table.

"I'm taking classes in music production, you know, just in case the singing thing doesn't work out."

"That can be a lucrative field," Lionel offered. "I have a friend who worked on the latest production by the Chicago Symphony Orchestra."

Who asked you? Maeve's lips itched to voice this opinion. Because of Charlie, she kept it to herself.

Charlie placed down a carousel of spreads for the bread, then straightened and rattled off the luncheon specials. Normally, Maeve would have jumped all over the herb-crusted beef tenderloin but she questioned whether she could get through the meal without throwing up. She'd bypassed breakfast and had been looking forward to the moment. Seeing Lionel had taken away her appetite.

"I'll have the farm salad," she said.

"Oh, come on, Wagyu beef is your favorite!" Lionel countered.

Maeve's look conveyed the opinion that, considering the time that had past, he had a lot of nerve acting as though he knew about her dietary preferences, or anything else.

"Or it used to be, anyway. What about the lobster, or baby back ribs? This is a chance to stick it to me, you know. Lunch is my treat."

"In that case, I'll have a dozen of everything on the menu." She delivered this request to Charlie with the straightest of faces. "Not really," she added, much to the waiter's relief.

"I'm not very hungry and have a dinner engagement." Thinking of Victor gave Maeve some much-needed strength to get through this unexpected ex-love reunion. "The salad is all I want."

"I'll take the tenderloin," Lionel said. He smiled at Maeve. "This isn't exactly a celebration, but it's been a long time. Could I interest you in a bottle of wine?"

"You're right. This is no celebration."

The door had barely closed on Charlie's backside before Maeve spoke. "Bruce. That's your middle name."

Lionel nodded.

"Where did Parker come from?"

He had the decency to look embarrassed. "*Karate Kid*."

One of their favorite movies. They saw it the week of Maeve's sixteenth birthday.

"Add that deception to the mile-long list of things for which you may never forgive me."

"It's actually a short list, Lionel. Lying to me then and lying to me now."

"I never lied to you, Maeve. I was madly, desperately in love with you."

"So much so that you ran off with another woman. I don't need anyone in love with me like that."

"There's so much you don't know."

Maeve looked at her watch. "I've got an hour. Why don't you tell me?"

"I got tricked."

Maeve arched a brow.

"You remember the Fourth of July weekend I went to DC with the family, to help my dad celebrate George's fiftieth birthday?"

"You didn't tell me the occasion."

"I couldn't. If I had, you would have wondered about not being invited." He sighed. "It's because George wanted me to be Hazel's date."

"Your wife."

"She was, is, George's oldest daughter, almost twenty-three at the time and with no real prospects for marriage. You're the most beautiful woman I've ever seen. Hazel is more average, back then overweight, and as a result suffered from low self-esteem. Dad asked me to escort her as a favor to his best friend. At the time, I thought it was no big deal, except the part about not telling you, of course.

"The festivities lasted all weekend. That Saturday morning is when I learned that Dad and George had a little more in mind than just my escorting Hazel to the party. Turns out George had been eyeing me as a potential husband for his daughter for quite some time, especially once I announced my plans for medical school. As for Dad, well, you know how into politics he is. He was the Point's mayor then with an eye toward becoming a senator and later governor, or more. Hazel's dad is one of the most well-connected men in all of the nation's capital. A marriage between her and I would create a powerful family dynamic."

"They spelled it out to you, just like that, and you went for it?"

"Of course not! My plan was to marry you, and Dad knew it."

"So how were you tricked?"

"That Saturday night during the main event of the weekend, someone spiked my drink. One minute I was on the dance floor, the next I was waking up in Hazel's bed. We were both naked. I didn't remember anything but she swore we had sex. Offered what looked to be a used condom as proof."

"Looked to be? You say that as though you're not sure."

"I hadn't brought any condoms with me. There was no need. Anyway, two months later, Hazel called to tell me she was pregnant. She told her father, who of course told mine, demanded we get married and quickly so that his daughter's reputation would not be ruined. Everything after that went by in a blur. The planning. The small yet elaborate ceremony on the island of Turks and Caicos."

"What about the honeymoon? Do you remember that?" Maeve wanted to kick herself for wanting to know, but had asked anyway. Couldn't help herself. Guess she wasn't as *over it* as she'd like to believe.

"I'd already lost you," Lionel pleaded. "I guess I was just…"

"Trying to make the best of a bad situation?"

"I didn't know what else to do. My thought was to stay with her throughout the pregnancy and then orchestrate a private divorce."

"Why didn't you?"

"She lost the baby. Shortly after moving into our dream home, she lost our first child."

"How convenient."

Maeve immediately felt like a cad.

"I'm sorry, I shouldn't have said that."

"Don't apologize. I had my doubts, too. So much so that I did a bit of investigative work and couldn't find one record of her as a patient in all of Prince George's County, DC, or the entire east coast. She came up with some cockamamie story about a private doctor and doulas and what not, one that her parents wholeheartedly co-signed. I still didn't believe it. But then Hazel went into a deep depression, one she couldn't possibly fake. It lasted for months. Compassion replaced anger. Eventually I began to care for her. And then, about a year later, she got pregnant again."

"I heard about that, the birth of your son."

Maeve's voice was soft, as the pang of hurt from that memory flitted through her heart. She was the one who'd planned to have Lionel's children. It was their family they'd discussed for years, the one they'd raise together in Point du Sable.

"His birth changed everything," Lionel admitted. "It was also right around that time that my dad got elected to the senate and I got approached to partner in a practice specializing in neuroscience with a good friend of Hazel's brother. From the day our doors opened we were booked solid, especially with athletes and ex-military fearing the onset of CTE."

"What's that?"

"Chronic traumatic encephalopathy—repeated physical trauma to the brain. Life settled into a routine. Then a year after Justin's birth, our daughter was born."

Lionel pulled back the cloth from the basket of rolls and leaned forward to sniff them. "I used to dream about these," he said, placing one on a bread plate and added a generous amount of maple butter before taking a bite.

He closed his eyes and moaned. Maeve knew the reaction was no exaggeration. Boxes of the club's rolls were often overnighted across the country and around the world. To know how delicious they were and not have the stomach to taste one was testament to just how much seeing Lionel affected her.

She took a sip of water. "I still don't get it. Whether or not Hazel tricked you into marriage, you stayed even after losing that child. Got her pregnant with two more. And then you abandon the family by divorcing them? Look, I'm no fan of your ex-wife. She destroyed what was supposed to be my life. But two wrongs don't make a right."

"They're not my biological children."

"Not your children? What the hell does that mean?"

Over the next half hour, he answered that question. Once finished, Maeve was almost sorry she'd asked. Remembering what had happened to Desmond, a situation that involved another baby surprise, made her more empathetic to his plight than she otherwise might have been.

"It's terrible what happened to you, Lionel. No man deserves what you've been through."

The food arrived. Lionel changed the subject by pulling out his wallet and showing Maeve a photo.

Her jaw dropped. "Our prom picture? Seriously, Lionel? After all these years?"

"I've carried it in every wallet I've ever owned since that night. It was a very special one, as you might remember."

Maeve's smile was bittersweet. "How can I ever forget?"

"I want you back," he said, after pouring his sad story all over Maeve's heart, taking her down memory lane and pointing out that aside from his horrendous betrayal, one for which he vowed to spend his lifetime making up, their good times had far outweighed the bad.

"I want us back. I was robbed of a future that should have belonged to us. It's all my fault. Had I the chance to do it over again, I would have stood up to my father, ignored my mother and left Hazel after the miscarriage despite the pressure to stay. When I learned you hadn't yet married, I knew it was a sign from God that all was not lost. That there was still a chance for our happily-ever-after."

"Life's not that simple, Lionel. I just… I don't know what to say."

"Then don't say anything. At least not now. Consider giving me a slow yes instead of a fast no."

"I'm seeing someone," she offered.

"I don't see a ring."

"It's new, but already my feelings for him run deep."

She watched Lionel's Adam's apple bob as he swallowed. "Thirty days, Maeve, that's all I ask. Give me, us, thirty days to see if the love we had can be rekindled. In all the years I was married to Hazel, my love for you never died."

Lionel's eyes glistened. Maeve had a soft spot for manly tears. She steeled herself against them.

"Please, thirty days. And if after that you still say we're over, I won't bother you ever again."

"I'll think about it," Maeve finally answered.

Lionel smiled as one lone tear slid down his face.

Damn. The last thing Maeve needed to do was start feeling sorry for the guy who'd broken her heart. She reached for her purse and stood abruptly.

"I've got to go."

Lionel stood as well. "I'll walk you out."

"It's okay."

"Actually, I took a car service here and was hoping you could give me a ride to PDS Medical Center."

Maeve looked at her watch. "Sure."

They reached the lobby area. "Can you give me a sec," Lionel asked. "I've got to use the restroom."

"Make it quick."

She leaned against the wall and casually checked emails.

"Hello, beautiful."

The voice caused a jolt to her punany. "Victor, what are you doing here?"

"About to demolish Cornelius in a game of tennis."

"Okay, honey, let's go."

At the sound of Lionel's voice, Maeve's head whipped around. Caught up in the Victor Vibration, she'd totally forgotten they'd just shared lunch.

"Is this one of your colleagues?" Lionel asked, looking from her to Victor. He lifted a hand toward Victor, while straightening to make full use of every one of the five feet ten inches the good Lord gave him. No match for six-four, but he tried.

"Hi. I'm Dr. Lionel Young."

Victor looked borderline amused as he returned the handshake with a grip that were it any tighter could have crushed the neurosurgeon's delicate fingers.

"Victor Cortez."

Victor answered Lionel without taking his eyes off her. Maeve realized she was staring back at him as though he were the Adam to her Eve, the peanut butter to her jelly, the hot butter to her breakfast toast...and that Lionel was watching. She wanted to avert her eyes but couldn't help it. The electricity between her and Victor still crackled, but that something had shifted could not be denied. That Victor felt it showed in his eyes.

"Some grip you got there, buddy!" Lionel said, adding a new level of bass to his voice. "Did you play football or basketball?"

This time Victor did look at Lionel. "Tennis. Polo."

Lionel's brow raised. "How do the two of you know each other?"

In every way imaginable and some we made up!

The way Victor smiled caused Maeve to believe their thoughts were similar and wary of what might come out of his mouth.

"He's Harvard," she blurted before he could speak.

"Ah," Lionel said, in a drawn out manner, as though her reply explained it all. "Well, it's nice to meet you."

"Is it?"

A level of new understanding played across Lionel's face. Before he could inquire further, however, Cornelius came through the club's revolving door.

"Hello, Maeve." They hugged. "Victor, I see you've met the brilliant surgeon taking the medical industry by storm. How are you, Lionel?"

"Good, good. Maeve and I were just leaving."

Leaving, yes, that would be a good thing, the best of all worlds, really. Because continued close proximity to Victor might bring out more of Lionel's curiosity and make her instantaneously combust. They reached the car.

Once inside, Lionel turned to her. "Maeve, my darling, nothing means more to me than winning you back. I'll do anything, everything, whatever it takes."

The seven-minute ride to PDS Medical was both the longest and the quietest of Maeve's entire life. Enough time for her to replay what had just happened, and realize that forgetting the past and embracing the future would be easier said than done.

Twenty-Four

Victor considered tonight a special occasion, his first visit to Maeve's house. He dressed casually but with care: off-white suede slacks, striped wool sweater and a pair of custom-made Tims. His curls were freshly cut, his face clean-shaven, his nails buffed, all courtesy of the spa at the Ritz, where he'd stopped after his lackluster game with Cornelius. All afternoon, his friend acted strangely. Was distracted during their matches. When casually mentioning the doctor, Lionel, Cornelius's response had been vague. His behavior suspicious, Victor's mind had immediately gone to Maeve's equally strange behavior earlier that morning, and to the ex that was back in town. He'd just as quickly dismissed the notion that Lionel was the man they'd discussed. Maeve had been adamant about not wanting to revisit her past.

Once in his car, all weird behavior was forgotten. Victor's mind had turned to making Maeve feel special. After placing an order with a jeweler he'd found online, he felt the plan complete. He'd wanted something as original and lovely as the woman who'd captured his heart. It was fairly common to bring flowers when meeting a date. Victor hoped the one he chose with diamond-dripping petals would meet with his lady's approval.

His lady. When had Maeve gained that status, moved from counselor to cutie-pie that he wanted to claim as his alone? Victor wasn't sure and just for tonight he wouldn't allow himself to think about it. He wouldn't go down the list of what-ifs, or recall all the failed relationships he'd either witnessed or experienced. He wouldn't set up the fence around his heart or let the tape of his father's voice play in his head.

You can't trust women. They'll let you down.

Treat women like royals, son. Keep an heir and a spare.

His dad would say this, often with an arm around one of those spares he recommended, laugh at his own narcissistic joke and smack the woman's backside. Later, Victor would witness the collateral damage of such thinking, his mother—first sad, then angry—retaliating with her own vengeance, a move that would give his father the opportunity to tell Victor, *See son, I told you they can't be trusted.*

All this before Victor was ten years old.

Nearing the impressive gates of the Eddingtons' compound, Victor allowed himself the slightest moment to glimpse into the future and see himself a part of a close-knit family like the one Maeve enjoyed, with parents who still loved each other enough after thirty-five years to throw a party and then set sail on a two-week cruise.

"Good evening, sir," he said to the guard on duty.

"Good evening. How may I help you?"

"I'm here to see Ms. Maeve Eddington."

"Sure, one moment. May I have your ID?"

Victor reached for his wallet. "Wow, you guys really have it locked down over here, huh?"

"Security protocol, sir."

"No worries. I understand." He handed it over and watched as the guard placed a call. Victor pulled out his phone and sent Maeve a text. While waiting for a response, he idly tapped the steering wheel to the beat of Bob Marley playing in the background, looking around at what he figured was some of the priciest real estate in the Midwest. Viewing the rolling hills and tall pine, oak and maple trees, his mind drifted to his home in Costa Rica, and how proud he would be to invite Maeve's close-knit family to his elaborate spread.

Maybe after her birthday celebration, depending on how things go...

The music continued. "Get Up, Stand Up" faded into "One Love." Victor's brow creased as he glanced at his watch. What was the guard doing? A background check? He looked over at the man still on the phone.

"Excuse me. Is there a problem?"

He held up a finger, finished the call and then walked back over to the window, holding out Victor's ID.

"Sorry about the delay, sir. A text has been sent to your phone with the GPS instructions to reach Ms. Eddington's home." The guard gave a curt nod and tight smile. "Enjoy your evening."

Victor wasn't used to waiting for anything, was one of those behind-the-velvet-rope kind of brothers. The delay had dampened his mood, but he tried to shake off the cha-grinned feeling as he neared Maeve's home. He parked in the drive, right next to the walk that led to a flight of stone steps, a cobble-stoned porch and an elaborate set of double doors. After gathering his coat and the gift bag for Maeve, he trotted up the steps and rang the bell. With dinner slated to be enjoyed in bed, how would she greet him. Sexy dress? Lingerie? Birthday suit?

None of the above. Maeve opened the door wearing a pair of scruffy jeans and a tee. She ran a hand through al-ready disheveled hair and attempted a smile.

She leaned against the door. "Hi, Victor."

The chagrin returned. Her mood seemed reminiscent of this morning, the one she'd admitted was fueled by the return of her ex. He crossed his arms. "Am I interrupting something?"

Her eyes fell to the gift bag, now swinging beneath his

arm. It was like a lightbulb went off, and she remembered inviting him to her house.

"Of course not. I'm sorry. I've been…preoccupied." She gave his arm a squeeze, then stepped back. "Please, come in."

A table was positioned a few feet inside the foyer. Victor set down the gift bag, reached for Maeve and pulled her into his arms. She stiffened at first, then melted into him, her body fitting his like it had been designed that way.

"I've wanted to do this all day."

She squeezed him tighter. "I've wanted you to do this all day."

Victor held her, felt her heartbeat, ran a hand through her hair. He wanted to kiss her, make love to her, but he thought of the earlier exchange with the doctor. His father's voice taunted him, the faces of women who'd deceived him in the past parading across his mind's eye. He needed answers. His arms dropped.

An awkward moment ensued. The first he could remember since that initial day at the club.

"Here, let me take your coat."

Victor handed it over. While she hung it in the hall closet, he retrieved the gift bag from the table.

"For you."

"Thanks, Victor."

Reaching for his hand, she led them into spacious living space with a two-story ceiling, matching chandeliers and an array of contemporary furniture in neutral tones. They sat on a couch facing the fireplace. She pulled the tissue paper from the top of the bag, unveiling a bottle of vintage French cabernet.

She took a moment to read the label. "I've never had wine from this region."

"It's supposed to be one of the best crops from their vineyard."

"And what's this? An aerator?"

Maeve pulled out a rectangular box. "Is this kid leather?"

Victor nodded.

"The box alone is a gift. It's beautiful."

"I hope you like what's inside."

Her gasp of awe was a clear indication that she did. She held up the platinum wine stopper adorned with a bouquet of flowers made from a variety of precious jewels.

"This is absolutely stunning, Victor. And so thoughtful." She leaned in for a light kiss on the lips. Despite his tangled emotions, Victor had other plans. He placed his hand at the back of her neck and pulled her in for a deeper exchange. She moaned, her hand slid across the soft sweater covering his toned torso and around his neck as she scooted closer and intensified the tongue dance. Soon, her hand slid down to his thigh, and over to his crotch. Victor felt himself expanding and knew that if the snake was let out of the cage, the night would go in a predictable direction and he may never get answers to the atmosphere he'd walked into when Maeve opened the door.

He ended the kiss.

"Wait." He looked into her lidded, startled eyes, and gave her swollen lips another quick peck before settling against the couch. "We need to talk."

"About what?"

"Your ex."

Maeve's flared nostril was the only indication of her surprise. "What about him?"

"Did you see him?"

She didn't answer. Victor braced himself for the lie that if his father were right about women would surely come out of her mouth.

"Is that why it took so long to get buzzed in, or why your greeting seemed tempered, your mind somewhere else?"

"He was my noon meeting."

"The doctor?" Maeve nodded. "Why didn't you tell me at the courthouse?"

"Because I didn't know it then."

His face conveyed his disbelief.

She sighed, reached for the wine bottle. "Have you tried this?"

He shook his head. "It came with high recommendations."

"Let's have a glass."

Without waiting for an answer, she stood and left the room. Victor leaned forward, elbows on knees, chin in hands, looking around Maeve's perfectly appointed space. It very much suited the woman he knew, especially the hodgepodge of colorful abstract artwork that emitted energies of discord but somehow matched. On one wall was a high-rise console table that held beautifully framed pictures of her family—Maeve and her siblings, her parents, all of them together. In another frame, an older couple beamed at each other. Grandparents, he presumed. There were pictures of young children, and one of her dressed to the nines and holding an award plaque. He was about to get up for a closer inspection when Maeve returned with an opened bottle and two wineglasses. He was immediately transported back to a similar scene, snowed in on top of a mountain, alone in their own magical world.

Maeve sat back down beside him and poured a small amount in the glass nearest her. She swirled around the liquid, closed her eyes and inhaled deeply before taking a sip.

"Um, that's amazing."

Victor simply nodded. She filled their glasses. He lifted his and clinked the one she held midair.

"Cheers," she said simply.

We'll see, he thought.

For the next few seconds, each of them thoughtfully sipped the excellent vintage. Victor watched Maeve. Maeve stared at the fire. After another deep sip, she sat down the glass but continued looking straight ahead.

"When Lionel made the appointment, he tricked my assistant by using a fake name. I went to the club to meet who I thought was a new client. He knew if he'd told the truth, I would have never gone. When I realized it was him, I almost left right away."

"Why didn't you?"

"I knew we'd have to talk eventually. It seemed silly to run. He's not only an ex but a friend to my family, a man whom I've known practically my whole life."

Victor shifted to see Maeve's whole face and better gauge her emotions. "How'd that go?"

"Not good, actually. Seeing him again, hearing his side of things, it was all very draining. It stirred up a lot of emotions long buried, ones I thought I'd worked through and, I don't know, thought could no longer affect me."

"Seeing your state of mind when you opened the door, they obviously did."

Another sigh, deeper this time. A bigger sip of wine.

"What was his story, his excuse for dumping you?"

"Thanks for putting it so bluntly."

"Isn't that what happened?"

"Yes." Maeve set down the glass, slowly paced the room as she shared the earlier exchange.

"He was tricked into marrying her," she began.

"Right…"

"I know. I didn't believe it, either. Not at first. She got pregnant."

"Oldest trick in the book."

Maeve relayed how Lionel claimed the night they slept together was a drunken blur with no memory of doing the act. "She miscarried, which caused Lionel to question if she'd even been pregnant. Her grieving seemed real, though, and led to depression, which brought them closer. Their son was born a year later and a daughter not long after that."

"Sounds like the trick worked out for him, at least for a while."

Maeve came back to the couch. "The children aren't his, Victor."

"What does that mean?"

"Turns out Hazel had a longtime boyfriend much as Lionel and I had been, one of which her parents would never approve. From the wrong side of the tracks, so to speak. She married Lionel to satisfy her parents but never stopped seeing her boyfriend. He, not Lionel, is the father of her children."

"How'd he find out?"

"The daughter began having difficulty breathing. The doctor initially chalked it up to allergies, then bronchitis. When neither of those diagnoses proved correct, and unbeknownst to either of them, he conducted a DNA test for further analysis and concluded she had asthma, something that doesn't run in either of their families. Lionel, suspicious once again, took a DNA test of his own. It was conclusive proof that he is not the father to either child."

"That had to be tough."

"He was devastated. Angry. The lie almost ruined their fathers' thirty-plus year friendship. Even after learning the truth, his wife and her parents tried to convince him to stay married. For the sake of appearances is what he thought, but they insisted it was because of the children. His senator father wanted them to stay married, too, but his mother encouraged him to follow his heart."

"Let me guess. His heart leads back to you."

"He tried several times to contact me after the initial breakup. Desmond blocked him."

"Good man."

Conversation stilled. Only now did Victor hear the subtle sounds of jazz playing in the background.

"You can't be thinking of going back with him."

"It's complicated."

"He was engaged to you but married someone else. What don't you understand?"

Maeve reached for his hand. "I have deep feelings for you, Victor, deeper than I've felt for anyone, even Lionel. But…"

"But what?"

"We dated for many years and would have married except for Hazel's deception."

Victor pulled his hand away. "What exactly are you saying?"

"He wants a chance to make it right. He asked me to give him thirty days…"

Victor stood. "Then clearly we're done here."

"Please, Victor, wait!" Maeve stood to catch up with Victor's long strides toward the front door. "I didn't give him an answer. I'm sorry but I've been blindsided. Him coming back was totally unexpected. I'm in shock, confused…"

"My coat, please."

Maeve pulled the leather trench from the hall closet. "I understand why you're angry but please, I just need to work this out."

"And what am I to do in the meantime?"

He waited. Maeve didn't seem to have an answer for that.

"Do you love him?"

"No! I don't think so. I don't know."

"Goodbye, Maeve."

Maeve stepped up to hug him. He held up a halting hand, then continued down the hallway, opened the door and stepped out on the porch. Small flakes swirled around him. He didn't feel a thing.

"Victor."

He felt her hand on his back and stopped. "I… This weekend was amazing. The wine stopper is exquisite. I don't want us to be enemies, or this to be over. I'll… I'll call you, okay?"

Victor had heard enough. He took the steps and strode toward his car. His father's voice trailed him. Mocking, laughing. Looks like Arly had been right, after all.

Twenty-Five

"I've ruined everything."

It was Tuesday morning, following Maeve's disastrous start to the week. She'd called her siblings for an emergency meeting. They were all there—Desmond, Jake and Reign—enjoying one of Chef's Southern-style breakfasts while hearing Maeve's woes. She'd come clean about her feelings for Victor, told them the details of her lunch with Lionel and ended with how Victor had walked out on her last night without a backward glance.

"That's a lot to handle in twenty-four hours," Reign said, a head full of waist-length braids twisting with the shake of her head. "I can't believe Lionel's nerve."

"Did you not get what happened to the brother?" Desmond asked. "He was tricked into leaving Maeve and marrying Hazel."

"Correction. He may have been tricked into the marriage, but he left me on his own."

"Via a breakup text," Reign added, as though Maeve needed more salt on that wound. "Let's not forget that."

Jake shook his head. "How could she with you continuing to bring it up?"

"Thanks, brother. Although you're right, Reign."

"He had his reasons," Desmond said.

"Whose side are you on?"

"Your side, sis, always. But I always thought you and Lionel were the perfect combination. And while I was extremely upset at what happened, especially how he handled your breakup, I never doubted his sincere love for you."

"So I heard." Maeve worked to keep a growing anger out of her voice.

"Doesn't mean I was always for you two getting back together. When it first happened, I dared him to contact you. I had witnessed firsthand how devastated you were about it. He was married. End of story. I didn't see anything good coming out of him reaching out."

"And now you're his biggest fan."

"Sis, I just believe that in his heart, Lionel's a good man. I also know how devious women can be, how someone can end up in a relationship with a woman because of a child when he had absolutely no say in the matter."

The table quieted as all remembered Desmond's drama with an ex-girlfriend before marrying Ivy, the true love of his life.

"When did you and Victor get so serious?" Jake asked. "I didn't even know y'all were dating."

"They were together over the holidays," Desmond replied with a look of consternation in Maeve's direction. "Must not be dating too seriously since she felt the need to hide."

"First of all—" Maeve reached for another helping of fresh fruit for her pancakes "—I'm grown. Secondly, my father's name is Derrick, not Desmond. I don't owe you an itinerary or an explanation."

She softened her tone. "To answer your question, Jake, Desmond's right. Victor invited me to his home over the holidays. We had a great time together in Costa Rica, but things really got serious this past weekend when Victor and I ended up snowed in together."

"I knew it!" Desmond tossed down his napkin. "He's got you sneaking around right under our noses?"

"She's not sneaking," Reign interjected. "I knew all about it."

"And didn't tell me?" Jake stabbed a piece of meat on Reign's plate and ate it. "Traitor."

"Do Mom and Dad know?" Desmond's look still judged her.

"Look, Victor isn't why I'm having problems right now. It's Lionel and his rather nervy and inconsiderate attempt to guilt trip me into giving him another chance."

"Love doesn't make you feel guilty," Reign said.

"I think you should do it," Desmond countered. "What's a month in the grand scheme of things? Given the circumstances and the length of time the two of you were together, I think you owe him that."

Jake scooted his chair away from the table and stood. "I think I'm going to get to work and mind my business." He leaned over and kissed the top of Maeve's head. "It's your life, sis. Nobody can live it but you."

By the weekend, Maeve was no closer to making a decision about Lionel but she had decided on one thing—to stop asking others for their opinions. Even without them, the past, like quicksand, was pulling her back into her old life. A group of friends had invited her to a party. She had no doubt Lionel would be there. Wouldn't put it past him to have orchestrated the gathering. But you only turned thirty once and she and Joycelyn had been on the same debate team in high school. They used to be close. Maeve hadn't seen her in forever. A lot of old friends would more than likely be there. Plenty of people to act as buffers between her and her ex. If only there was something to block her constant thoughts of Victor. She'd reached out to him several times— both professionally, regarding an email from the judge that he'd also received and personally, saying she missed and was thinking of him. Even ended the last text with x's and o's. He hadn't responded. Not. Once. She told herself it didn't matter. It did matter. A lot.

That night as Maeve dressed for the party, her heart wasn't in it. She would have been fine in jeans and a sweat-shirt, but knowing the importance of dressing the part of a successful professional, she dug through her wardrobe for a form-fitting burgundy sweaterdress maxi with matching leather boots. Her fluffed curls bounced around her shoulders as she got into her car and headed to Homer Glen, a tony suburb of Chicago where the private mansion Joycelyn had rented out was located. She played reggae and thought about Victor the whole ride over. By the time she pulled up to the valets dressed in red jackets and black slacks, her stomach roiled. Tonight would be the first time seeing Lionel since the lunchtime invasion and the asinine give-me-thirty-days request from the man who'd shattered her heart into a trillion pieces and reentered her life at the exact moment when she'd met another man able to put it back together again. Even in this social setting—with trusted friends who had her back, including some who knew what happened—Maeve felt vulnerable, almost nauseous. She told herself that she was overthinking the situation, that Lionel was her ex not the big bad wolf, and that Victor wasn't the only whale in the ocean. He was probably the finest, smartest and sexiest one swimming around, but there were others.

When the valet approached and opened her car door, she put on a bright smile, gave her hair a toss and headed up the steps to the wide veranda that wrapped around the fifteen-thousand-square foot, Tudor-style mansion. She was familiar with the neighborhood, yet it was her first time at the ultra-high-end home often rented by the super rich and famous, and others who could afford to walk around in that world. She entered a massive foyer, impressive even to a child who'd grown up in the lap of luxury and a world of wealth. The chandeliers were as large as merry-go-rounds and sparkled against the gleaming mahogany floors. Familiar faces flitted about, carrying flutes of champagne and tumblers of Scotch. Seeing her friend Regina, she smiled and headed over.

"Hey, girl," she greeted before air-kisses.

She was surprised when Regina pulled her into a hug.

"Lionel's here," she angrily hissed, then stepped back, all smiles and shimmers.

"I figured he would be."

Regina's eyes widened. "You knew he was back in town?"

"Just found out."

"And I didn't get an immediate phone call because…"

"Mostly because I've been trying to forget all about him, especially after accidentally meeting him for lunch this week."

Regina grabbed her arm and began pulling her down the hall. "We need to talk."

"We really do. So much has happened."

"Obviously."

Their convo would have to wait. Marilyn, Toy and Angie, three friends who Maeve hadn't seen in years, bumrushed them, all oohs and ahhs over Maeve's sleek look.

"You haven't aged a day," Angie said, three kids in four years having caused huge changes in her once-petite frame.

"Did you hear Lionel got divorced?" Toy asked.

"No way!" Marilyn stopped a passing waiter and snatched a flute from his tray. Maeve followed suit, almost took two. To endure the night, she might bribe one for a bottle.

"I hear he's back in Point," Toy said. She looked at Maeve. "Did you know that?"

Toy had always been the friend stirring up drama. The roiling in Maeve's stomach increased.

Already planning an exit strategy, Maeve thought to set the foundation for the gossip she was sure would follow in her wake.

"I heard he'd returned, though it's really not my business. I hate that his marriage didn't work out and hope that he's able to recover and find another, as I've done."

Where had that declaration come from?

She avoided Regina's look of surprise and noted Toy's eyes widen, almost dancing with glee. "Do tell, girl. Don't keep us in the dark."

"A girl never kisses and tells," Maeve coyly answered. She looked up to see Cornelius and Peyton walking toward them. She gave them a smile.

Toy sucked in a breath. "Cornelius? Who's he with?"

"Hey, ladies!" After a round of introductions and a minute of chitchat, he turned to Maeve. "Can I talk to you for a minute?"

"Sure." She turned and took in a variety of expressions, including Regina's disappointed one. "I'll call you," she whispered, and then to the rest said, "See you on the dance floor."

"Cupid Shuffle?" Marilyn asked.

"Absolutely!"

Cornelius led her beyond a double staircase in a living room easily holding at least a hundred people and over to a small alcove boasting two wingback chairs and a round marble table. They sat down.

"How are you doing?" His voice oozed concern.

"I'm okay."

"Did Victor call you?"

"No. I've been trying to reach him but haven't heard back."

"I know he's been traveling. But I'm surprised he didn't let you know."

A family of butterflies took up residence in Maeve's stomach. "Let me know what?"

"That he's no longer representing the Duberry estate."

Maeve relaxed a little. "The case has been dismissed."

"Not in Adele's mind. She still believes a large chunk of their inheritance was stolen."

"She needs to talk to her brother," Maeve mumbled.

"What's that?"

"Never mind."

"At any rate, Victor called me last week and asked if I would take over the case. I can't, especially now that we're planning a wedding, and all."

"Oh, my gosh, that's right! Forgive my forgetfulness. Congratulations! Reign told me that you and Peyton had gotten engaged."

Cornelius blushed. "Yes, we're very excited."

"I'm truly happy for you, Cornelius."

"Thank you." He looked just beyond her. "Looks like we're about to have company."

A swarm of butterflies encircled her stomach. She didn't have to turn around to know who approached.

"Well, look what the cat dragged in!"

Cornelius stood and greeted Lionel. Maeve stood, too.

"Maeve!" Lionel turned with arms outstretched. "What a sight for sore eyes!"

"It's good to see you," she said, and was surprised that she meant it. Maybe it was the champagne, but in the moment she didn't despise Lionel as she had at Monday's lunch. No matter what happened in the future, in the past this man had been her world. She may not ever again be in love with him, if she ever was, but she would always feel a type of love for him.

While returning his embrace, she noticed something that hadn't been there before. Muscles. His body wasn't as toned as Victor's but was definitely harder than when they used to hug on the regular.

She stepped back. "Have you been working out?"

Lionel flashed that lopsided smile that at one time had flip-flopped her insides. Today's reaction was much more subdued.

Duly noted.

"While in DC I took up weight training," Lionel admitted, clearly proud that his stronger, more toned body had been recognized.

"Don't get cocky, Doc," Cornelius said. "Those muscles will melt away quickly if you don't hit the gym."

"Don't I know it."

"Cornelius, who's now handling the case?"

His attention returned to Maeve. "Patrick."

"I'm surprised he didn't call me."

"He's probably intending to. Everything just happened this week."

"Uh, no." Lionel stepped between them. "What we're not going to do is talk shop tonight. We're here to celebrate Joycelyn." His eyes softened as he looked at Maeve. "And I'm here to ask this beautiful lady to dance."

Maeve didn't want to embarrass him with an outright refusal so she linked arms with Cornelius and they entered the dance hall together. Later, she'd thank the gods because the moment they stepped into the room, the popular song encouraging line dancing began to play. The floor quickly filled with people going right, left, kicking and walking by themselves.

She stayed for two hours, danced and dined with her friends before giving Joycelyn her birthday gift and quietly slipping out as the Stevie Wonder rendition of "Happy Birthday" bounced off the walls. She'd enjoyed herself, but even more, she'd realized that the past was the past and there was no going back to it. There was, however, unfinished business to handle involving her future. On the way home, she called Victor again. No answer, but this time Maeve left a clear, succinct message:

"I never took you for a quitter." Then she turned up the volume in her car as a Bob Marley tune began to play.

He didn't call that weekend. Or the next week. Lionel had called regularly. Mostly they went to voice mail, but when he rang her the Friday evening before her birthday, she took the call.

"Hello, Lionel."

"Hey, stranger! You're hard to reach. What are you doing?"

"Just chilling, flipping through a magazine."

"You're at home? On a Friday night?"

"Guilty as charged."

"We can't have that. How'd you like to go into the city, maybe take in a movie. Or visit that new neo-soul club that's all the rage. Or both. What do you say?"

"I say no, Lionel."

A pause and then, "Okay. We don't have to do anything special. How about I just come over for a game of chess. You do still play, right?"

"Not in a while. But that's not a good idea, either. I am glad you called, though."

"That's good to hear."

Probably not after what I have to tell you. "I've made a decision, Lionel. There will be no thirty-day trial or revisiting our past relationship. That part of our lives is over. I loved you for a long time and hope we'll always be friends. But my heart belongs to someone else. And it's past time I let him know it."

The night before Maeve's twenty-ninth birthday, she boarded a plane bound for Costa Rica. She hadn't heard from Victor but his silence hadn't stopped her. She was determined to hold court, force him to hear her argument, and if she was granted her birthday wish, win the case she'd present hands down.

Twenty-Six

Victor was in a mood. Not a good one. After spending a few weeks back home in Puerto Limon, he'd made business trips to Tanzania and China. During those travels, he'd ignored Maeve's calls, texts and emails. Yet, he'd thought of her daily—okay, sometimes hourly—had even begun dialing her number a few times before changing his mind and ending the call. Why? Because history had proven that no matter how he felt with Maeve in his arms, the relationship would not end well. His father had repeatedly told him that the happily-ever-after only existed in movies. In his third marriage, Victor's father believed it impossible to be faithful to only one woman. So far, until Maeve, Victor had found that to be true. His dad had also told him women couldn't be trusted. One minute, he and Maeve were talking about the future. The next, she was *confused* and vacillating due to a blast from her past.

In all fairness, it wasn't just Maeve. The time apart had given Victor the chance to reevaluate the situation, question whether or not a longtime commitment was in his blood. His father didn't think so. But some of Cedella's blood also flowed in his veins, and when it came to his mother, Victor had never observed one more loyal. He had a feeling that, once in a relationship, Maeve was like that. She wasn't the type of woman with a heart you played with. He'd observed her parents and their family, saw a closeness and synchronicity that he'd never witnessed firsthand. Sure, he was feeling her now but what about six months from now? A year later? What would happen if he set out and made a promise that he couldn't keep? What happened in Chicago hurt like hell but in the end may have probably been best.

"Victor?"

"What!" He closed his eyes, grit his teeth and took a breath. "I'm sorry for snapping, Hasina. Must be the jet lag."

"You've been home for three days."

"The change in time zones, then."

"Pick an excuse you can live with and I'll believe you. Meanwhile, the band has arrived. Where on the boat should they set up?"

Victor bit back a curse word. He ran a frustrated hand over a jaw covered with day-old growth. "I told you to cancel all that."

"I'm sorry, Victor. In the hoopla surrounding the christening of my grandbaby, I clearly forgot."

Victor took a deep breath and reined in harsh emotions. "It's okay, Hasina. How was the service?"

Hasina visibly relaxed. "Beautiful! Would you like to see pictures?"

"Of course."

Hasina left and returned with a small photo album. "The baby looks like Leandro," he said.

"He has her nose," Hasina admitted. "But the rest of that pretty face is all me."

"No resemblance to the parents?" he asked with amusement.

Hasina leaned in to study a photo. "Maybe a little."

Leandro entered the room. "Sir, the chef is ready to board the yacht and would like to speak with you regarding the menu. Should I convey your wishes, or would you like to do so yourself?"

"No, you can take care of it. Whatever the chef suggests is fine." Victor looked between two people more like grandparents than employees. "What would I do without you two?"

"Get in a world of trouble most likely" was Leandro's immediate reply.

"You're probably right. Tell you what. You guys deserve to enjoy a beautiful night. Hasina, why don't you go up and put on one of those fancy Sunday dresses? Leandro, don one of your good suits. I'm giving the two of you the night off. The yacht is yours, to enjoy a wonderful dinner and an evening of dancing."

"Oh, Victor. I— We couldn't do that." Hasina reached up and placed petite hands on either side of Victor's face. "You made all those plans for you and your sweet lady."

He gently removed her hands. "There's no more me and sweet lady, but the night might as well not go to waste. I suppose you didn't cancel the fireworks, either."

"I'm sorry. Everything is scheduled to go as you planned, but Leandro and I can't go on the boat. Not unless you agree to come with us."

"Hasina, I've never been a third wheel a day in my life. I will not start tonight."

"Okay, fine. If you insist."

"Thanks for not being stubborn for once in your life."

"We'll go on one condition."

"What's that?"

"That after the band gets set up, you'll at least join us for a glass of wine."

"I guess I can do that."

"Okay." Hasina and Leandro turned to leave. "See you in an hour?"

Victor nodded. "An hour. One drink."

"And please, dress appropriately. If we have to pull out our Sunday best, then it's only right you do so, too."

An hour later, Victor smiled as he straightened the eighteen-carat gold-threaded tie, courtesy of the Ace collection by his friend and famed designer out of California, Ace Montgomery, married to an equally famous model, London Drake. Hasina would have a hissy if she knew that the slip of material being knotted around his neck had set him back six figures. With only two other such ties in the world, Victor knew the collector's item would only increase in value. If he ever had grandchildren who got in a pinch, the sale of it could buy them a house or put them through college.

He stood back from the mirror and eyed his reflection. He'd decided to don the dark gold suit he'd had Ace tailor for what he thought would be a private birthday celebration. The suit fit him to a tee, emphasized his wide shoulders, vee waist, slim hips and tight ass. The gold threads in the tie winked out from their black background, further highlighted by a black shirt. He slipped bare feet into a pair of Gucci loafers and, after a swift brush of his curly coils, set out the short distance to the slip where the boat was moored that would take him out to the yacht.

"Evening, Jimmy," he said to the strapping lad operating the boat. "How's the family?"

"Everyone's fine, sir."

Victor got on the boat and sat on a middle board, placing a hand on each side of himself for balance. The boy started up the boat and headed to the twinkling lights on the yacht in the distance.

"How did Leandro and Hasina enjoy the ride over?"

Jimmy hesitated slightly before answering, "Um, fine, sir."

Victor let it go. Hasina was afraid of water and had probably chided the boy for the ocean's waves. They reached the yacht. One of the crew immediately secured the steps used for boarding. Victor greeted the crew, shook hands with the captain and then began walking toward the light sounds of reggae music played by the band. Caribbean music always made him feel better. His bad mood dissipated further with every note. He was glad he'd agreed to join his workers for a glass of wine. Heck, he had nothing else to do that night. He might have two.

He turned the corner. Stopped. Blinked. Thought he was dreaming. Prayed that he wasn't.

If I am, please, don't wake me up!

Maeve had never seen anyone look so delectable. So delightful. So desirable. So delicious. It took every ounce of willpower she had and some that she borrowed to not make like a projectile and shoot herself into Victor's strong arms. In that moment, the feelings she had for Victor versus any other man were as plain as black-and-white. Spending a lifetime with someone safe like Lionel, instead of someone like Victor who felt like a soul mate, would not only be unfair to the man but to herself. She didn't want a nice happy life, where the fires burned low and steady but never burst into a roaring fire, a passionate inferno that took her breath away, the way Victor's intense gaze was doing to her right now.

He took a step closer to her, his face void of expression. "What are you doing here?"

"Pleading my case, Counselor. Since you refused to return any other mode of trying to reach you, I came to present my argument in person."

"That's pretty bold, don't you think? I could have been out of the country or…otherwise engaged."

"You could have. But you're not."

"No, I'm not."

"No, you're not."

Maeve knew good and gosh darn well she sounded like a parrot right now, but the redundant comment bought her a couple seconds to look for sanity and find a modicum of composure before losing all discipline, crushing her lips against Victor's and humping his finely spun wool-covered pant leg.

"You invited me here for my birthday, remember?"

"I remember a lot of things."

Said through a set of lips that should require a license to

carry. Lord, the man was about to make her swoon like an eighteenth-century maiden whose bone corset was pulled way too tight!

His eyes narrowed, roamed her body. "Where's Lionel?"

"Not here, nor anywhere I care about."

"What happened to him wanting a month to plead his pitiful case?"

"I refused him. I don't need a month, or another second, to be clear on one thing. Lionel was my past. I hope you are my future."

He reached out and ran a single finger down her arm. She flinched as though burned, swearing she could feel his heat through her clothes. Victor's face split open with that cocky, knowing smile, the one that caused certain muscles to clench and for moisture to pool in intimate places.

"Tonight, will you be my birthday gift?"

His eyes dropped to her lips as she asked the question. Her heart threatened to dislodge itself from her rib cage and drop to her stomach. In fact, given the steady thrumming of her vagina, it may have already fallen even lower than that.

"There you go, wanting to use my body again."

"Among other things."

She took a step to claim a kiss but was interrupted.

It was Hasina. "Ah, so you found her!"

Victor whipped around. He looked from Maeve to Hasina and back. "Wait, you knew about this?"

Hasina's chin lifted. "I did." Clearly, she was unapologetic, even proud.

"That's why you didn't cancel anything."

Hasina looked at Maeve. "I always knew he was smart."

"It's my fault, Victor," Maeve explained. "I contacted them, asking for help."

"Begging," Hasina jokingly clarified. "I couldn't refuse her."

Victor took a step toward Hasina, fixing his face into a

playful frown. "You know, just because you've known me since before I was born doesn't mean you can't be fired."

"Yes, it does. It also means that if you mistreat this beautiful lady, I can box your ears."

Leandro rounded the corner. "Hasina, can you please come on so that we can get off this boat? If you keep yapping, they'll never get married and we'll never see a grandbaby on these grounds!"

Usually, Hasina would have a smart comeback for her husband of several decades. Tonight, though, she simply smiled at Victor, winked at Maeve and walked out of the room.

"You and Hasina planned this ambush?"

"I didn't want to come all this way and find you gone."

"I could be angry with you, and it would be justified."

"You could, but you're not."

He leaned down for a gentle kiss on the lips. "No, I'm not."

Maeve exhaled. "Good."

The band was amazing. The dinner, delightful. Afterward, they took cups of spiked coffee to the bow of the boat to enjoy the breeze and take in the stars. Maeve again apologized to Victor, becoming vulnerable by revealing her deepest truth.

"I love you, Victor."

"Really?"

"You're surprised?"

"Not long ago, you were considering another man's thirty-day plea."

"I never really considered it. You already had my heart."

"When did that happen?"

"Honestly? That first magical night here in Costa Rica. But it wasn't until getting snowed in at Hotel Bouvó that I knew for sure."

"Why didn't you tell me?"

"Given past heartbreaks, it isn't easy for me to admit being in love. Still, you're worth the risk.

"Do you love me?" she asked, her eyes wide and searching. "Don't answer that. It's probably too soon to ask."

Victor set their cups on a table and pulled her into his arms.

"I'm crazy about you, that's for sure. Still, it's going to take more than looking good and smelling nice to totally win me over. You've made quite the declaration but, Counselor, I think we'll have to retire to the bedroom before hearing the rest of your argument, and presenting my response."

Maeve sidled up to him and placed her arms around his neck. "I'm ready to proceed with my case, and just so you know, I plan to win again."

A crackling sound caused them both to turn just as bursts of color erupted overhead. The pyrotechnics were dazzling but the two barely saw them. They were too busy looking at and kissing each other, ready to create hot and heavy fireworks of their own.

* * * * *

#2917 RANCHER AFTER MIDNIGHT
Texas Cattleman's Club: Ranchers and Rivals
by Karen Booth

Rancher Heath Thurston built his entire life around vengeance. But Ruby Bennett's tender heart and passionate kisses are more than a match for his steely armor. Anything can happen on New Year's...even a hardened man's chance at redemption!

#2918 HOW TO CATCH A COWBOY
Hartmann Heirs • by Katie Frey

Rodeo rider Jackson Hartmann wants to make a name for himself without Hartmann connections. Team masseuse Hannah Bean has family secrets of her own. Working together on the rodeo circuit might mean using *all* his seductive cowboy wiles to win her over...

#2919 ONE NIGHT ONLY
Hana Trio • by Jayci Lee

Thanks to violinist Megan Han's one-night fling with her father's new CFO, Daniel Pak, she's pregnant! No one can know the truth—especially not her matchmaking dad, who would demand marriage. If only her commitment-phobic, not-so-ex lover would open his heart...

#2920 THE TROUBLE WITH LOVE AND HATE
Sweet Tea and Scandal • by Cat Schield

Teagan Burns will do anything to create her women's shelter, but developer Chase Love stands in the way. When these enemies find themselves on the same side to save a historic Charleston property, sparks fly. But will diverging goals tear them apart?

#2921 THE BILLIONAIRE PLAN
The Image Project • by Katherine Garbera

Delaney Alexander will do anything to bring down her underhanded ex—even team up with his biggest business rival, Nolan Cooper. But soon the hot single-dad billionaire has her thinking more about forever than payback...

#2922 HER BEST FRIEND'S BROTHER
Six Gems • by Yahrah St. John

Travel blogger Wynter Barrington has always crushed on her brother's best friend. Then a chance encounter with Riley Davis leads to a steamy affair. Will the notorious playboy take a chance on love...or add Riley to his list of heartbreaks?

Get 4 FREE REWARDS!

We'll send you 2 FREE Books plus 2 FREE Mystery Gifts.

FREE Value Over **$20**

Both the **Harlequin® Desire** and **Harlequin Presents®** series feature compelling novels filled with passion, sensuality and intriguing scandals.

YES! Please send me 2 FREE novels from the Harlequin Desire or Harlequin Presents series and my 2 FREE gifts (gifts are worth about $10 retail). After receiving them, if I don't wish to receive any more books, I can return the shipping statement marked "cancel." If I don't cancel, I will receive 6 brand-new Harlequin Presents Larger-Print books every month and be billed just $6.05 each in the U.S. or $6.24 each in Canada, a savings of at least 10% off the cover price or 6 Harlequin Desire books every month and be billed just $4.80 each in the U.S. or $5.49 each in Canada, a savings of at least 13% off the cover price. It's quite a bargain! Shipping and handling is just 50¢ per book in the U.S. and $1.25 per book in Canada.* I understand that accepting the 2 free books and gifts places me under no obligation to buy anything. I can always return a shipment and cancel at any time by calling the number below. The free books and gifts are mine to keep no matter what I decide.

Choose one: ☐ **Harlequin Desire**
(225/326 HDN GRTW)

☐ **Harlequin Presents Larger-Print**
(176/376 HDN GQ9Z)

Name (please print)

Address   Apt. #

City   State/Province   Zip/Postal Code

Email: Please check this box ☐ if you would like to receive newsletters and promotional emails from Harlequin Enterprises ULC and its affiliates. You can unsubscribe anytime.

Mail to the **Harlequin Reader Service:**
IN U.S.A.: P.O. Box 1341, Buffalo, NY 14240-8531
IN CANADA: P.O. Box 603, Fort Erie, Ontario L2A 5X3

Want to try 2 free books from another series! Call 1-800-873-8635 or visit www.ReaderService.com.

---

*Terms and prices subject to change without notice. Prices do not include sales taxes, which will be charged (if applicable) based on your state or country of residence. Canadian residents will be charged applicable taxes. Offer not valid in Quebec. This offer is limited to one order per household. Books received may not be as shown. Not valid for current subscribers to the Harlequin Presents or Harlequin Desire series. All orders subject to approval. Credit or debit balances in a customer's account(s) may be offset by any other outstanding balance owed by or to the customer. Please allow 4 to 6 weeks for delivery. Offer available while quantities last.

Your Privacy—Your information is being collected by Harlequin Enterprises ULC, operating as Harlequin Reader Service. For a complete summary of the information we collect, how we use this information and to whom it is disclosed, please visit our privacy notice located at corporate.harlequin.com/privacy-notice. From time to time we may also exchange your personal information with reputable third parties. If you wish to opt out of this sharing of your personal information, please visit readerservice.com/consumerschoice or call 1-800-873-8635. **Notice to California Residents**—Under California law, you have specific rights to control and access your data. For more information on these rights and how to exercise them, visit corporate.harlequin.com/california-privacy.

HDHP22R2

HARLEQUIN
PLUS

Announcing a **BRAND-NEW** multimedia subscription service for romance fans like you!

Read, Watch and Play.

Experience the easiest way to get the romance content you crave.

Start your **FREE 7 DAY TRIAL** at
<u>www.harlequinplus.com/freetrial</u>.